SHOWDOWN WITH A LOW-DOWN SNAKE

Lancaster suddenly gave a shrill whistle.

Just as suddenly, eleven of his men appeared. Some stepped out from behind trees. Some rose from behind boulders where they had been crouching. All were armed either with rifles or revolvers. All their guns were aimed at either Ki or Jessie.

"I'm so sorry you didn't see fit to accept my business proposition, Miss Starbuck," Lancaster said as he began to raise his left hand.

He's going to signal his men to begin shooting, Jessie thought. She glanced at Ki.

Understanding passed between them although no words had been spoken.

Jessie fired a round that had been deliberately aimed to go over Lancaster's head. It caused him to drop his arm and go for his gun. . . .

WESLEY ELLIS

LONE STAR

ON THE WARPATH

JOVE BOOKS, NEW YORK

LONE STAR ON THE WARPATH

A Jove book/published by arrangement with
the author

PRINTING HISTORY
Jove edition/July 1989

ISBN: 0-515-10062-5

Jove books are published by The Berkley Publishing Group,
200 Madison Avenue, New York, New York 10016.
The name "JOVE" and the "J" logo
are trademarks belonging to Jove Publications, Inc.

PRINTED IN THE UNITED STATES OF AMERICA

10 9 8 7 6 5 4 3 2 1

★
Chapter 1

"What an absolutely marvelous morning!" Jessie Starbuck exclaimed as she rode up onto a ridge and into the bright light of the just rising sun. "Look, Ki," she cried, pointing. "The sun seems to be turning those clouds over there into pure gold!"

The handsome young man riding beside Jessie nodded, yawned, and looked in the direction she had indicated. "It looks as if the world is just being born," he remarked in a resonant voice that was in no way harsh. "Everything looks brand new."

"It's absolutely beautiful," Jessie murmured, awed by the brilliance of the sunrise that was gilding everything within sight and turning lurking shadows into broad vistas of shimmering loveliness.

They rode down from the ridge, two pilgrims moving into the beginning of a bright new day, both of them exulting in the sunlight and crisp May-morning air, which was as refreshing and heady as a properly aged wine.

Jessie's coppery hair caught the light and reflected it. The clear light made her green eyes glisten and gave a golden glow to the smooth skin of her face.

Jessie was a woman of average height, but the litheness of her figure and her evident air of self-confidence tended to make people think she was taller than she actually was. Strikingly attractive, she was a woman who turned the heads of men wherever she went. A woman who had, either wittingly or unwittingly, *over*turned the yearning hearts of many men.

She wore jeans that seemed to cling lovingly to her long lean legs. Her blue cotton blouse, although loose-fitting, could not entirely disguise the lush bloom of her full breasts. Over her blouse she wore a black leather vest and around her neck she had tied a red bandanna. On her head was a flat-topped Stetson with a chin strap.

The half-Japanese, half-American Ki riding beside her had hair as black and glossy as her leather vest. It was ramrod straight and shoulder-length. His eyes were the color of acorns and very slightly slanted, a subtle indication of the Oriental blood that flowed in his veins. But his height of nearly six feet bore impressive testimony to his Caucasian heritage. At first glance, many people did not identify Ki as an Asian. Those who did usually and mistakenly assumed he was Chinese.

His body, like Jessie's, was lean and strong, a body made of much muscle and little fat. But unlike Jessie's flawless skin, Ki's showed signs of weathering. There were faint lines at the corners of his eyes, and two others that ran from his nostrils down to the sides of his thin-lipped mouth.

Like Jessie, he too wore jeans, the seat of which was shiny. The cuffs were also showing signs of wear. He wore them over the shanks of his high-topped black boots. His tan shirt was of checkered cotton. In the pockets of his brown leather vest rested eight potentially deadly *shuriken*, or martial arts throwing stars, each of which had five blades sharp enough to slice into wood. Or flesh and bone.

"There's the cow camp," he said, pointing toward the horizon where a thick swirl of smoke from a cooking fire rose lazily into the air. Cowboys stood around the fire while not far away a herd of cattle quietly grazed. "I hope we're not too late for breakfast. I'm hungry enough to eat half a horse. No, a *whole* horse."

2

"I told you you should have had something to eat before we left the ranch. It's no wonder that you're hungry now."

"You didn't give me time to get anything to eat. You had me awakened long before dawn, and then you hustled me out here without so much as a by-your-leave."

"That's not true, and you know it isn't," Jessie countered with a smile. "But even if it were true, you should be grateful to me for getting you up and out here in time to see the glory of the sunrise."

"Salt pork all crisp and juicy," Ki said dreamily, licking his lips. "Biscuits from a hot Dutch oven dripping butter. Boiled beans. If the men in that cow camp of ours have eaten everything, I swear I'm going to lie down, roll over, and die of starvation."

When they rode into the camp some time later, they were greeted by a slender man with a sunburned face and rawboned body.

"Morning, Miss Starbuck," he called out. "Howdy, Ki."

"Good morning, Ed," Jessie said as she got out of the saddle and dropped her reins. "How are you?"

"Just fine, Miss Starbuck. Fine and dandy. Didn't expect you quite so early. Thought you'd likely be along later in the day."

"I wanted to get an early start," Jessie explained. "Are we going to be in your way showing up this early?"

"Oh, no, not a'tall. The boys have still got a bit of branding to do but that shouldn't take too long. Then we'll bunch up the herd and move it out."

"How many head will you be driving up to Indian Territory?" Jessie asked.

Before Ed could answer her, Ki spoke up. "Ed, is there by any chance any food left over from breakfast? I'm as hungry as a bear coming out of hibernation."

"The boys, they've mostly eaten by now," Ed replied, "but there's likely to be some vittles left. We had rice and raisins with sugar in the mix this morning and some cornbread that was as tasty as a young girl's kiss."

Jessie smiled as Ki heeled his horse and headed for the chuck wagon, which was parked in the shade of a tall locust tree.

Ed pulled a tally book from his pocket and flipped through its pages. "To answer the question you asked me a minute ago, Miss Starbuck—let's see here now—we'll be trailing two hundred and fourteen head up to the Cheyenne and Arapaho reservation this time. I can tell you true that each and every one of 'em's fit as a fiddle and fat as a housecat."

"The winter grazing was good then, I take it?"

"It was just fine. The weather favored us this winter. Not much snow and what did fall didn't last. So the beeves got to eat their fill without having to do too much foraging. Course they'll lose a little flesh on the drive, but they'll gain it all back and then some once they're put to pasture on the land we've leased up there in the Nations."

"How many men are you taking with you on the drive?"

"I reckon we'll take along seven men not counting me, the cook, and the wrangler. That's two men to ride point, two swing, two flank, and one unfortunate fellow to ride drag. The rest of the outfit'll head over to Sweet Valley and move the stock that wintered there on up into the hills for the summer.

"Miss Starbuck, I know that's nearly twice as many men as Bob Statler took when he left for the leased land on the reservation a month or so ago. But Bob had only about half as many head to nurse along, so—"

"Ed, you take as many men as you need to get the job done properly," Jessie interrupted. "You know I'm not one to cut corners at the expense of doing a good job."

"I know you ain't, Miss Starbuck. I just thought that maybe you might have felt like I was taking along more men than the job called for."

"Ed, you've worked for the Circle Star ranch now for two years, isn't it?"

"Yes, ma'am, two going on three."

"During that time you've done an excellent job, and I want you to know I appreciate it. It's men like you who make Starbuck Enterprises the successful operation that it has been and continues to be."

"Thank you for the kind words, ma'am. Have you had any word from Bob Statler?"

"No, I haven't, although it has been his custom in the past to contact me by telegraph once he's sold our Circle Star stock in Dodge City."

"He was supposed to do like we're going to do, am I right? I mean Bob was going to drive cattle up to the leased land on the reservation and pick up already fattened cattle there to sell in Dodge?"

"Yes, that's right."

"It's funny you haven't heard from him. Why he must have reached Dodge days ago. You don't suppose he ran into any trouble along the trail, do you?"

"I hope not. Perhaps he was delayed. Or perhaps he decided not to send a telegraph message to me this time. Bob's a very reliable man. I'm sure I'll be hearing from him sooner or later."

Ki returned carrying two plates heaped high with the rice-raisin mixture and cornbread Ed had mentioned. He handed one of the plates to Jessie.

"Looks to me like you forgot to get yourself some eating irons, Ki," Ed observed and then headed for the chuck wagon.

"I was so hungry, I forgot all about cutlery," Ki confessed to Jessie. "All I could think about was food, not how to eat it."

When Ed returned and handed knives and forks to Jessie and Ki, she told him, "I had a telegraph message yesterday from Jeff Marsden. He said he has nearly two hundred head waiting for you to drive to Dodge once you get this bunch up on our leased land."

"How are things on the reservation these days?" Ed asked as Jessie and Ki proceeded to eat standing up. "Any trouble with the Cheyennes or Arapahos?"

"Not as far as I know," Jessie replied between mouthfuls of food. "At least, Jeff didn't mention any trouble in his telegram."

"I know it's a good deal for Starbuck Enterprises to lease land on the Cheyenne and Arapaho reservation to graze stock on," Ed drawled, thoughtfully stroking his chin. "But it always did, and I reckon it always will, strike me as a tricky, not to mention a risky proposition. Those Indians, they could turn on the cattlemen leasing land from them quicker'n you can say 'Listen to the whippoorwill.'"

"I suppose that's true enough," Jessie mused, devouring the last of her cornbread.

"But the Cheyenne and Arapaho have been living peacefully on the reservation for some time now," Ki interjected. "Should there be any Indian trouble, there's an army over at Fort Reno assigned the job of keeping the peace and putting down any disturbances on the reservation."

"I know. It's just that I don't trust a one of 'em though," Ed persisted. "Those Injuns would as soon take your hair as bid you good day. In a way, I reckon you can't blame them for doing such dastardly things. They've been kept down in the dirt for so long that, why, hell—beg pardon, Miss Starbuck—they wouldn't be human if they didn't want to stand up on their hind legs and hit back at all the white folk who've been hitting so hard on them for so damn long. Beg pardon, Miss Starbuck, I'm just not used to having women around this here cow camp."

Ki took Jessie's empty plate and cutlery along with his own back to the chuck wagon. As he was about to turn and rejoin her and Ed, a cowboy lounging beside the wagon's possibles drawer called out, "Hey!"

Ki glanced in the man's direction. "Were you calling me?"

"Are you her cook?" the cowboy inquired.

"I beg your pardon?"

"Her," the cowboy repeated, ramming a thumb in Jessie's direction. "You must be her cook since you certainly ain't her fiancé. Miss Starbuck of the Circle Star ranch surely wouldn't keep company with a China Boy."

Ki walked away. He was halfway to where Jessie and Ed were still engaged in conversation when the cowboy caught up with him, laid a hand on his right shoulder, and spun him around.

"How come you don't answer when I talk, China Boy?"

"It's because I don't think I have anything to say to you."

"*Hooeeee!*" hooted the cowboy. "Don't you talk fancy though!"

Ki calmly but firmly removed the man's hand from his shoulder. As he turned to leave, the cowboy stepped in front of him, blocking his path, his hard hands solidly planted on his bony hips, his close-set eyes glinting with a fiery light.

"What's she like, China Boy, your high and mighty mistress. Is she hot, huh? Come on, you can tell old Lem."

"Lem," Ki said in a cold voice, "I'll tell you this. A snake who likes to bite had better make sure his fangs are sharp."

"Oh, mine are plenty sharp enough to take on a lousy half-blood like you."

Fury exploded within Ki, but he forced himself to hold it in check. "I would appreciate it if you would say nothing more about Miss Starbuck in my presence."

Lem thrust his head toward Ki and muttered, "You say I'm not to mention that Starbuck lady's name around you.

7

Now, do you really think you're man enough to tell me what to do and what not to do?"

"I think so."

"And make it stick?"

"Yes, and make it stick."

Lem suddenly swung a fist, and his roundhouse right knocked Ki to the ground. As he fell, Jessie came running toward him, followed by Ed.

Ki lay on the ground, supporting himself on his elbows. As he stared up at Lem, a crowd of cowboys began to gather around the pair.

"That's enough!" Ed yelled when he arrived on the scene. "Lem, you get on back to work."

Lem ignored the order. To Ki, he said, "Heard you were some kind of hand-to-hand fighter. It don't look to me though like you could go hand-to-hand with a gnat, never mind a man like me."

Jessie was about to bend down to help Ki to his feet, but he waved her away and rose in one swift fluid movement to his feet. He kept his eyes on Lem, sensing the man's mood, divining the man's next move. When it came, he was ready for it.

As Lem's left fist swung up toward Ki's chin in a somewhat awkward uppercut, Ki reached out with both hands. He grabbed the man's fist, spun in place, bent forward, and threw Lem to the ground.

The cowboy hit hard, and the thud he made was audible as was the sibilant rush of air from between his thick lips.

Ki stood, his body perfectly balanced, his mind engaged in practicing the *ninja* art of *kime*, the focusing of concentration on the matter at hand—in this case, on his would-be enemy. A casual observer of Ki would have thought, mistakenly, that he was merely observing his downed opponent. In fact, he was readying himself for the attack he was anticipating. Every cell and nerve in his body was primed not only to respond to that expected attack but also to survive it and emerge from it the victor.

Lem growled something unintelligible, and a serene but keenly alert Ki saw the gleaming knife the cowboy drew from its sheath in his boot.

Ki took a single step backward as Lem got gracelessly to his feet, knife in hand, anger twisting his features.

"Back off!" Ed yelled and made a move toward Lem, but Jessie whispered something to him and restrained him by placing her hand on his forearm. He gave her a dubious look but remained where he was beside her.

Lem lunged at Ki, the knife in his right hand slashing in a wide arc parallel to the ground.

Ki waited until the arc had reached its point of no return without having touched him. Then he stepped swiftly forward, seized his attacker's right wrist, pivoted his own right wrist counterclockwise, and struck Lem's right wrist a savage blow with his right hand, causing the cowboy to drop the knife.

Ki's right hand continued moving upward, all five fingers stiff and outstretched. He struck Lem a sharp blow on the neck, while simultaneously checking the man's right arm with his left forearm to keep it neutralized.

Moving his right hand clockwise now, he struck Lem's throat with a hatchetlike blow that caused his opponent to gag and stagger backward. He stepped back as Lem, clutching his throat, fell to his knees and began to retch.

Ed stepped forward and picked up Lem's knife, which he thrust into his belt. "You had enough, mister?" he barked at the still-retching Lem. "Get on your horse and get out of here. You're through as of right now!" He threw a gold eagle into the dirt beside Lem who looked up, saw Ed towering over him, picked up the coin, pocketed it, and rose. Cursing, he staggered away, and within minutes he was aboard a bony roan and riding south away from the cow camp.

"He's a bad one," Ed muttered, shaking his head in chagrin. "I never should have hired him. But he told me a tale of woe fit to break the heart of a stone, so I took him on two days ago against my better judgment. Did he hurt you, Ki?"

"No."

"What was that all about?" Jessie asked Ki.

"Bad manners," he answered.

Jessie was about to pursue the matter but something about the look Ki gave her dissuaded her from doing so.

"All right, you boys have better things to do than stand around here gawking," Ed said to the crowd of cowboys who had been watching the encounter between Ki and Lem. "Build a fire somebody, and let's heat up the branding irons."

The men began to disperse, some them casting admiring, even awed, glances at Ki. One of the cowboys, a grizzled veteran, declared to a younger companion as they walked away from the fight scene, "That there Ki can fight smooth as silk and mean as a cat with its tail caught in a crack."

"Ed," Jessie said, "I've brought the money you'll need to pay the men off at the end of the drive as I promised you I would. It's in my saddlebag. I'll get it."

"I swear, Ki, I never can get over those moves of yours," Ed said when Jessie had gone. "I declare they were slick as shit on a stick."

"I learned the martial arts in Japan when I was younger," Ki replied, "before coming here to this country to work for Jessie's father. My *sensei* was a very wise man and a most skillful teacher."

"Your what?"

"*Sensei*," Ki repeated. "It is a Japanese word. It means master. In a literal sense, it means 'one who is born before'."

"You mean your master, he was older than you."

"Yes, that's right. But the literal translation doesn't necessarily refer to a master's chronological age. It can refer, and very often does, to the master's wisdom which makes him, in spiritual terms, the student's elder even though the student may actually be older than his master."

"You lost me somewhere back around the last bend," Ed said with a grin. "But I saw enough of you in action to know that whoever your master was and whether he was older or younger than you at the time, he sure must have been hell on the hoof if he could teach you to do like you just done to that scoundrel, Lem."

"What are you two talking about?" Jessie asked as she returned with a gunny sack in her hand.

"I was telling Ki he's one man I'm sure not going to meddle with . . . ever," Ed said, his grin broadening.

"He can take care of himself quite well, can't he?" Jessie asked, casting a frankly admiring glance at Ki.

"He sure can do that well enough," Ed agreed. "I reckon by now Lem has reached the conclusion that he bit off a mite more than he could chew when he challenged Ki. You knew he'd wipe the floor with Lem, didn't you, Miss Starbuck? That's why you kept me from stepping into the fight."

Jessie nodded and handed the gunny sack to Ed. "The money is all there. It will cover wages, supplies, any emergencies you might run into, and there's also a twenty dollar bonus as well for you and each of your drovers when you get to Dodge. That should help all of you to have a good time once the drive's over and done with."

Ed took off his hat and scratched the back of his balding head. "Miss Starbuck, I've never been known for having a way with words. But I would like to say that you're as generous as you are good-looking, and that's my way of saying you are one real generous lady."

"Why, Ed, I thank you kindly for the very nice compliment. Now, if you don't mind, I'd like to take a look at the stock. Can you spare the time to join me?"

"Be pleased to join you. Just hold tight here for a minute while I go see if my horse has woke up yet. Be back as fast as a turpentined cat travels."

Ed was as good as his word. He quickly returned aboard a buckskin gelding.

Jessie and Ki climbed into their saddles, and the trio rode out together, heading for the herd in the distance.

Behind them, a branding fire was now blazing, and the first of the steers had been roped by a cowboy who was dragging it bawling through the dust toward the fire where its road brand would be applied.

"That steer over there and the one over there," Jessie said as they rode the flank of the herd. "See them, Ed? The ones with the twisted horns? I think you'd do well to dehorn those two before you set out. They can do a lot of damage with those deformed horns in a tightly packed herd."

"I'll get the clippers and cut off their crowning glory my own self before we leave," Ed promised.

"What's your man doing over there?" Ki asked Ed.

"Beg pardon?" Ed yelled, his hand cupping his ear, because Ki's words had been drowned out by the loud bawling of a steer as a branding iron seared its flesh.

Ki shouted his question, and Ed answered it with, "That there's Spike Conroy, out unofficial veterinarian. We've had an outbreak of maggots in some of our beeves' branding wounds and also where they were . . ."

As Ed's words trailed away, Jessie said, "There's no need to be embarrassed, Ed. I've spent time around branding fires since I was a girl. You're saying that some of the cattle have become infected after having been castrated, isn't that right?"

"Yes, ma'am, it is," a blushing Ed replied.

Ki suppressed a smile.

"Spike's daubing the infected spots with a mixture of carbolic acid and axle grease, which works about ninety percent of the time," Ed explained. "Those maggots, they cause the animals awful agony, as you two no doubt know. They kill some of the beasts, and it's a real bad way to die.

"Spike—you see what he's doing now?—He's dousing that steer with kerosene. It's one of a small cut that's caught some sort of skin disease. Don't know for certain what it is. Something akin to mange only it ain't mange. Spike swears the kerosene cures whatever it is the critters have got. Kills chiggers and ticks too, which is a kind of bonus, I reckon."

They rode on then, Jessie's keen eyes roving over the cattle, checking the condition of the cows and their calves, noting the development of the yearlings, judging the Circle Star's stock breeding program by the results she was seeing. By the time they had completely circled the herd and were returning to the branding fire, she was generally pleased by what she had seen.

"They're looking good," she told Ed. "The increase is gratifying and so is the fact that those blooded Durhams we imported two years ago from the East are crossing well with out native longhorns."

"They are indeed," Ed agreed enthusiastically. "Just take a look at that bunch right there. You can see the two strains in them as clear as day."

"I can. They've got the strength and durability of the longhorns and the meatiness of the Durhams."

"They're not as vulnerable to heat and drought as the pure Durhams are nor are they as scrawny as a lot of longhorns are," Ki commented.

"I see the day coming," he added, "when cattle dealers in Kansas, and everywhere else for that matter, aren't going to pay nearly as much for a pure longhorn as they will pay for Western crossbreeds like we've been producing for the past year or so."

"Look out!" Ed yelled, and they all turned their horses sharply to avoid colliding with a steer that came careening toward them as it was pursued by a mounted cowboy whirling a grass lariat above his head.

"That steer is sure giving Parker a run for his money!" Ed cried gleefully as the steer began to widen the distance between itself and the pursuing Parker. "He don't relish having his hide tickled with no branding iron!"

Something about the steer bothered Jessie as she sat her saddle, flanked by Ki and Ed, watching Parker chase the animal. Its hide didn't look right to her. But what . . .

The answer to what was bothering her came to her as suddenly as did the sharp scent of kerosene that suddenly filled the air and then was as suddenly gone again. The steer, Jessie realized, was the one she had seen being doused with kerosene earlier as a treatment for its skin disease. In its wake had come the strong smell of kerosene in which its hide had been soaked.

"Go get him, Parker!" Ed yelled, standing up in his stirrups and waving his hat at the cowboy who was still chasing his quarry.

"Where are you going?" Ki called out to Jessie as she suddenly went galloping toward the fleeing steer. As she rode, she took a coiled rope from her saddle horn, fashioned a lariat and soon had a wide loop whirling about her head.

Too late.

The words echoed in her mind. She knew she was too late to cut the steer off. In its fright, it was continuing to run straight toward the fire. The cowboys around the fire, seeing the animal lumbering relentlessly toward them, dropped their branding irons and ropes, released the cow they had been about to brand, and fled in all directions.

Parker gained on the steer.

"Back off!" Jessie yelled to him, but either he didn't hear her or he chose to ignore her command. He continued

14

riding hard after the steer whose great eyes were wide with fright.

When the animal neared the fire, it abruptly seemed to recognize what was about to happen to it, but by then it was too late for it to avert the deadly danger. It tried but failed to swerve in time. Instead, it went plowing on and into the fire.

When it emerged from the fire a moment later, its body had become a torch. Flames rose from it, sending dense black smoke billowing into the air. The sickeningly sweet stench of burning flesh filled the air.

Jessie rode around the fire as a cowboy behind her shouted, *"Good bleeding Christ on the cross, he's heading for the herd!"*

She slammed boot heels into her horse, and the animal sped forward. Jessie kept her eye on the steer that was now screaming in agony as it ran on while its body continued to burn, revealing white bones that quickly charred. Judging her distance carefully, she used a sidearm cast to throw a heel catch that encircled the steer's hind legs and dropped it to the ground.

She took several swift dallies around her saddle horn and then drew rein. As her horse held its ground, she started to take a half hitch in her rope to lock it in place but it burned through and fell away from the steer's legs.

The animal, grunting, staggered to its feet. Fell. Tried to get up. Couldn't. It lay convulsing where it had fallen, the flames consuming it, no longer able even to give voice to its agony and terror. A moment later, it moved no more.

"You stopped that critter just in time!" Ed cried as he and Ki rode up to Jessie.

"He would have set fire to half the herd it he'd gotten to them," Ki added.

"I never knew he was going to do such a fool thing," Ed muttered. "How did you know, Miss Starbuck?"

"I recognized the steer as the one your man, Spike

15

Conroy, had treated with kerosene," Jessie answered. "I was afraid he might, in his fright, run blindly into the fire and then try to rejoin the herd if he could."

"Miss Starbuck," Ed said, "I've got to hand it to you. You think real fast and act even faster. If that animal had run into the herd, why, there's just no telling how many head we'd've lost. They'd've gone running this way and that, and we'd've had ourselves a barbecue we never once wanted."

Parker, the cowboy who had been pursuing the now incinerated steer in order to bring him to the branding fire, rode up. "Miss Starbuck, I sure am sorry about what happened. I never for so much as a single minute thought that critter would run right into the fire. If I had, I would have let him go on his merry way and gone after some other steer."

"You did what you thought best," Jessie said. "Sometimes when one does that, it doesn't always work out as planned."

"Like this time," a sheepish Parker murmured.

Jessie turned to Ed. "I'll be heading back to the ranch now. Have a good drive." She shook the man's hand.

"Thanks, Miss Starbuck, we'll try to," Ed said. "Thanks too for bringing out the payroll. I could have picked it up at the ranch on our way north."

"I was glad to do it. Frankly, I wanted to be out and doing on this loveliest of May mornings."

Ed shook hands with Ki and stood watching as he and Jessie turned their horses and rode away.

Jessie and Ki made their nooning on the crest of a hill that looked down into a valley that was filled with brilliant yellow buttercups nearing full bloom.

They ate brown bread and goat cheese, which Jessie had packed in her saddle bag before leaving the ranch that morning, and drank goat's milk from their canteens.

It was late afternoon by the time they arrived back at the Circle Star ranch.

"Looks like you've got company," Ki observed as they rode up to the front door near which a black surrey was parked.

"I wasn't expecting anyone," Jessie said as she dismounted and turned her horse over to Ki to take to the barn.

She entered the house to find a plump middle-aged woman sitting stiffly in a mohair chair in the middle of the great room beneath the portrait of Jessie's mother, which hung on the wall above the gray slate fireplace.

"Miss Starbuck?" the woman said, rising as Jessie halted in the doorway.

"Yes, I'm Jessica Starbuck."

"My name is Mrs. Ida MacKenzie, Miss Starbuck. Your housekeeper let me in. I've come about my boy, Billy."

"Your boy, Mrs. MacKenzie?"

"Yes. He works for you."

Jessie suddenly remembered the boy named Billy MacKenzie. "Won't you sit down?" she asked his mother. "Would you like some tea? Some coffee perhaps?"

Mrs. MacKenzie shook her head as she sat down again.

Jessie noticed the way the woman was nervously twisting a linen handkerchief in her hands. She sat down across from her visitor. "I remember your son very well, Mrs. MacKenzie. He's a very nice boy. Most mannerly, as I recall. And so very eager to be a cowboy."

"Actually, Miss Starbuck, what Billy wants to be is a man. He reckons cowboying might be the route to take to where he wants to get to."

Jessie smiled. "He told me he was fifteen. 'Going on sixteen' was the way he put it, as I recall."

"It was good of you to hire him. He came home all excited. He told his pa and me how he was fixing to be a wrangler on a drive up to the Nations and then on to Dodge

17

City, thanks to your kindness in taking him on. Miss Starbuck, I'm worried sick about Billy."

"I'm sure mothers always worry about their children when they leave home for the first time to go out on their own. But I hasten to assure you, Mrs. MacKenzie, that Billy is in very good hands. The trail boss on the drive of which Billy is a part is a man named Bob Statler. He is an experienced cowhand, and I specifically asked him to keep an eye on your boy. To take Billy under his wing, so to speak, and to teach him everything he could."

"I appreciate that, Miss Starbuck. But the reason why I'm worried is not because my boy has left home at such a tender age—I know boys like Billy can't wait to grow up and be independent—it's that I haven't heard a word from him."

"He hasn't written to you?"

Mrs. MacKenzie bit her lip and looked down at the handkerchief she was still twisting in her hands. "No," she said softly, "Billy didn't write. Billy doesn't know how to write, you see."

She looked up at Jessie. "Billy's pa made him promise before he left us to send us a telegram once he got to Indian Territory. But we haven't received one, and he should have reached Indian Territory by now, shouldn't he have, don't you think?"

"Yes, but I wouldn't worry unduly, Mrs. MacKenzie. It's possible that Billy couldn't get to Darlington to send the telegram as planned. He'll probably send one from Dodge City."

Jessie recalled her earlier conversation with Ed. He had mentioned that Bob Statler should have reached Dodge City days ago. This had led him to ask her if she thought Statler might have encountered trouble on the trail. A feeling of uneasiness crept over her.

"I came by, Miss Starbuck," Mrs. MacKenzie was say-

18

ing, "to ask if you have received word of any kind from your drovers since they left here."

"No, I haven't," Jessie admitted for the second disconcerting time that day.

"Mr. MacKenzie said that Billy should have gotten to Dodge City by now. But we didn't get a telegraph message from there any more than we did from Indian Territory. Billy has always been a good son to us. He doesn't lie, and he keeps his promises. He's mature for his years, Billy is. If he said he would send us a telegram then he would have sent one if it was humanly possible for him to do so. You can see, based on what I've just told you, why the Mister and me are so worried. We're sore afraid that something bad might have happened to our boy."

"I'm sure, Mrs. MacKenzie, that Mr. Statler would have informed me immediately if anything had happened to your son. But I can certainly understand your concern. I'll do what I can to try to ease your mind. I'll contact the Indian agent in Darlington and find out if the Circle Star drovers have been there and gone on, as I suspect they have. If such proves to be the case, I'll then contact Mr. Tom Breyer, who is the representative of the cattle company that buys our stock, to find out if they have arrived there with the cattle they would have picked up on our leased land and driven north."

"Oh, Miss Starbuck, I would so appreciate it if you'd do that. I know it's silly of me to worry so but—"

"It's not one bit silly, Mrs. MacKenzie. It shows how much you love your son."

"You'll let me know what you find out, won't you, when you receive replies to your telegraph messages? We live in Bear Hollow right close to Green Creek."

"I'll be in touch with you tomorrow unless there's a delay in receiving replies to the inquiries I intend to make. But I will be in touch just as soon as I have some information on the matter, I assure you of that."

"Thank you. Thank you ever so much."

After Jessie had shown Mrs. MacKenzie out, she stood alone in the great room, thinking about Billy MacKenzie and wondering why the boy had not contacted his parents as he had promised to do. Her feeling of uneasiness grew stronger, making her decidedly uncomfortable.

★
Chapter 2

Jessie recalled the day she had first seen Billy MacKenzie. It had been more than a month ago on a rainy April afternoon.

Ki had brought the boy to her and announced, "I found this stray mooning about outside, and all I could get out of him was that he wants to talk to you."

Jessie had asked Billy his name, and he had given it. Then she asked him why he had come to the Circle Star ranch to talk to her.

"If you please, ma'am, I'd like it fine if you could hire me as a hand."

"How old are you, Billy?"

"Fifteen going on sixteen."

"Do your parents know what you have in mind to do? What's more important, do they approve?"

"They know, ma'am. I told both pa and ma. At first they thought I might be too young, but I reminded ma how she got married when she was fifteen. Being married's a lot more risky than being a cowboy. I think that's what won her over to my side. Pa, though, he didn't come right out and say so at first, was on my side all along. He was a drover on the Chisholm Trail when he wasn't but a year or two older than I am now. He kind of likes to see me following in his footsteps is the way I figure it."

"Have you ever worked with cattle before, Billy?"

"No, ma'am, I haven't, but I've watched cowboys and

my pa. He's taught me a lot about how to care for stock. We have some of our own cows on the homeplace, and pa says I've got me a way with critters that no doubt comes from my ma who pa says can gentle even the fiercest of beasts if she puts her hand and mind to it and—"

"Hold on a minute, Billy," Jessie interrupted with an indulgent smile. "Do you ride?"

"Yes, ma'am, I surely do. I rode over here today to talk to you. My horse, he's hitched to the rail right outside. I could ride before I could walk. I was only hock-high to the first horse pa set me on."

"Rope?"

"Some. I'm not the best at roping, but I'm getting better."

"Can you stop a stampeding herd of cattle single-handedly?" Jessie asked, sure that Billy was going to swear to her, in order to get the job he wanted, that he could stop *two* stampeding herds single-handedly.

He opened his mouth to answer her. Closed it. Shook his head. Said sadly, "No, ma'am, I don't reckon I can do that."

"You can't?" Ki asked with exaggerated incredulity, playing Jessie's game with the boy who stood twirling his hat in his hands and studying the plank floor of the room.

"No, sir, I sure enough can't do a thing like that." He looked up at Jessie, brightening. "But maybe I could learn how to were somebody to take the time to teach me."

Jessie and Ki burst into laughter.

A puzzled Billy asked them, "Did I say something comical?"

"Never mind," Jessie said, sobering and feeling great affection for this sincere and eager young man who, she thought, would one day be a heartbreaker with his bright blond hair and deep green eyes.

"Let me ask you another question or two, Billy," she said.

The boy waited expectantly.

"If you were in charge of the remuda on a trail drive and you had your choice, would you keep the horses in your charge out on the open plain or in a stand of timber?"

"I'd take them out in the open, ma'am, even if I had to travel a far piece to do that on account of how there's lots of shadows in timber and some horses get spooked by them. What's more, there's bugs of all kinds and flies and the like, and they bother horses a whole lot. Out in the open there's likely to be less of them. What's more, if it's cat country you're in, why, the open plain is the best place to keep a remuda on account of how cougars like to lurk in timberland."

"Do you think you can handle a herd of as many as twenty or more horses by yourself, Billy? Now wait. Before you answer bear in mind that you not only have to handle them you also have to know their names and which cowboy each one belongs to."

"I have me a good memory, ma'am, so I reckon I could recollect which horse went with which cowboy. As for handling a herd of horses, I reckon I could do that. I would look out for horses who tend to head for home the minute your back's turned. Some of those bunch-quitters, they don't leave tracks enough to trip an ant, and once they turn tail and bid you goodbye, they can be as hard to find as a fly in a currant pie.

"I'd keep the remuda from drifting, but I'd loose-herd them. Horses don't much like to be held too tight together. It puts them off their feed."

"Billy, I think you would make an excellent Circle Star wrangler," Jessie declared solemnly.

"I agree one hundred and ten percent," Ki said.

"You mean . . . you're taking me on then?" Billy asked, his eyes dancing.

"You'll be joining a trail drive heading up to Dodge City in a week or so," Jessie told him. "You'll be in charge of

23

the remuda on that drive. The trail boss is a man named Bob Statler. He'll pay you forty dollars a month and found —if that's satisfactory?"

"Oh, ma'am, that's as satisfactory as can be! I thank you for taking me on. I'll do a good job for you. I swear to you that I will. I won't give you no cause to regret giving me this chance to start out on my career as a cowboy."

"Mr. Statler is with the herd on the plain below Devil's Hills," Jessie said. "Do you know where that is?"

"I do."

"Why don't you go there and introduce yourself to him and tell him I said you're to be his wrangler on the upcoming drive."

Billy had shaken hands with both Jessie and Ki, and then, once outside the ranch house, he had *yipeeed* his way aboard his horse and went riding hell-bent-for-leather toward the Devil's Hills and his new life as a fledgling cowboy.

Jessie was roused from her reverie by the return of Ki.

"You're frowning," he noted. "Is something wrong?"

"I don't know."

"What's bothering you? Something obviously is. Was it the visit of that woman I saw driving away just now as I came out of the barn?"

"That was Mrs. MacKenzie, Billy's mother."

"Billy's mother," Ki repeated and then, "oh, I remember Billy MacKenzie now. The boy who wanted to be a cowboy. The one you sent off to be the wrangler on Bob Statler's cattle drive."

"Mrs. MacKenzie hasn't heard from Billy, and she's worried. It seems he promised her and his father that he'd telegraph them from Darlington. But he didn't. Nor did he send a wire from Dodge City. Mrs. MacKenzie is afraid something might have happened to him."

"If something had, Statler would have notified you."

"I know. I told her that. I also told her that we would

contact the Indian agent at Darlington and ask if the Circle Star herd arrived there and moved on to Dodge. If he says it has, I promised Mrs. MacKenzie we'd then get in touch with Tom Breyer in Dodge to see if he has bought our stock. I said I would let her know what I found out."

"Do you want me to go into town to send the telegrams?"

"Would you? I'd go but I find I'm suddenly very tired."

"That's what getting up before dawn does to you," Ki teased. "Let that be a lesson to you."

When the smile he had elicited from Jessie faded, he added, "You're worried about the men ... about whether something went wrong on the drive, aren't you?"

"I am. I don't mind admitting it. When Ed first pointed out that Bob should have reached Dodge days ago, I felt a little uneasy because, as you know, Bob's been in the habit of wiring me from Dodge to let me know the terms of the sale he negotiated there. But I told myself it was foolish to worry. All sorts of things could have delayed the drive. Weather, for one. A stampede.

"Then, when I found Mrs. MacKenzie here waiting for me with the news that she had not heard from her son, well, I decided then and there it was time to look into the matter for her sake as well as my own."

Ki headed for the door. Before he reached it, he turned and said, "I may not get an immediate answer to my telegrams. If I don't, I think it would be best if I stayed in town until I do which may mean overnight ... or even longer."

"I'll see you when you get back."

As Ki opened the door, Jessie said, "There's one thing I forgot to mention. When you wire Darlington and inquire about the herd, please ask for word of Billy MacKenzie. Find out if he's all right."

"I'll do that."

• • •

Dusk was deepening into night when Ki rode into town and stopped in front of the General Mercantile that also housed the post and telegraph offices. He dismounted, wrapped his reins around the hitchrail out front, and went inside. He made his way over to the desk in a corner of the room where an elderly man with wisps of white hair escaping from beneath the green eyeshade he wore was busily tapping out a message.

When the man had finished what he was doing, he cocked his head and peered up at Ki. "Help you?"

"You can. I'd like to send a message."

Ki proceeded to fill out the form the man handed him, and then he handed it back to the telegraph operator who took it, peered at it, and said, "Darlington, Indian Territory,"—he peered some more—"That'll be a dollar and five cents."

Ki paid the fee and told the telegraph operator, "I'll be back to get the reply to that message. What time do you shut up shop?"

"Nine P.M. sharp."

"See you before then."

Outside, Ki looked up and down the street and chose the larger of the town's two saloons, the Golden Calf. As he cut a diagonal course across the street in the direction of the saloon, the wind shifted and he could smell the rank odor of the cattle that were being held in pens several blocks away next to the railroad station.

Upon entering the saloon, he found that the stench faded but did not entirely vanish. Instead it blended with the acrid odor of cigar smoke and cheap perfume emanating from the men and women crowding the noisy room. He made his way over to the mahogany bar where he found a place for himself and ordered whiskey.

When the bar dog had placed a bottle and glass in front of him, he poured a single finger of whiskey into the glass

26

and slowly sipped it, turning as he did so to survey the crowd.

Several couples, one of them composed of two trail hands, were dancing to the music of a fiddler who was being accompanied by a man with a banjo. They shuffled merrily through the sawdust covering the floor, which was stained in places by tobacco juice that had never made it into the bent and battered spittoons placed here and there on the floor next to the walls.

Ki's eye fell on one buxom blond who, he decided, couldn't be called a beauty but who also wasn't ugly. Big breasts, bigger hips, and a mouth, he thought, that didn't get that big from sucking bananas.

When the fiddle and banjo music died, a dapper man wearing a derby, frock coat, and spats took his place in front of the instrumentalists, and the music began again, this time with the derby-hatted, spatted man launching into sly song:

> "When you are single
> And living at your ease
> You can roam the world over
> And do as you please. . . . "

Ki watched the big-breasted woman clasp her hands on her partner's buttocks. He continued watching as the woman neatly lifted the man's thin purse from his trouser pocket and just as neatly tucked it under a garter she wore beneath the short skirt of her green silk dress.

> "But when you are married
> And living with your wife,
> You've lost all the joys
> And comforts of life.
> Your wife she will scold you,
> Your children will cry,

27

And that will make papa
Look withered and dry. . . . "

Ki turned back to the bar and helped himself to some cubes of cheese which were resting on a plate near his elbow. After downing several pieces, he cracked the shell of a hard-boiled egg he took from a bowl on the bar, peeled, and ate it.

He was reaching for a second egg when a woman came running up to him. She took his arm, leaned over, and planted a wet kiss on his cheek.

"Ki, I haven't seen you in here in a coon's age!" she cried, her blond curls bouncing, her breasts doing the same. "I'd begun to think you were mad at little Lois."

"Honey, how could I get mad at a lady like you who knows just about all the ways in the world to keep a man like me happy and those ways she doesn't know she makes it her business to find out fast."

"You're not drinking that terrible house brand of booze, are you? That's no better than that Pass Whiskey they dish out in El Paso. There was a man in here the other night who—I swear this is the gospel truth—took a jolt of that whiskey and it stopped his watch, snapped his suspenders, and cracked his glass eye clear across!"

"That well may be, Lois," an amused Ki responded, "but me, I'm made of sterner stuff. It won't do me any harm, and it just might do me some good."

"Sterner stuff, huh?" Lois repeated, giving Ki a wink. "How about *stiffer* stuff?"

"Lois, you do have a way of getting right to the point."

"This is the point I want to get to, and don't you just know it though?" Lois began to grope Ki.

Looking at her pert lips, her smooth skin, her buxom body and feeling the heat of her hand through his jeans as she continued to fondle him between the legs, Ki grew almost instantly erect. He stayed that way, throbbing with

28

lust and longing for this rowdy woman he had bedded several times.

"Your fee," he said huskily. "It's still twelve bits?"

"It is. But forget my fee. This one's on the house. I'm turning the old saw around tonight: pleasure before business. You ready to go?"

Ki was as ready as he would ever be. He left his unfinished drink on the bar along with the money to pay for it and let Lois take him by the hand and lead him across the room and through the batwings.

As they emerged into the darkness outside that was only partially dispelled by flickering gas lamps, Lois turned and started across the street.

"Aren't we going the wrong way?" Ki asked her. "The Hotel Deluxe is down that way."

"I moved. Or rather the management asked me to move one night last week. It seems that one of my customers took exception to a drunken soldier who wanted to horn in on us. There was some shooting. Nothing serious. Two windows broken. There was some fighting. Nothing serious. A bureau and chair broken. But they told me I had to vamoose. The manager of the hotel got a real bad case of the hives as a result of the disturbance. He has a nervous condition, as I understand it. Gets Saint Vitus Dance from time to time, and there's no holding the man down when he does. So now I'm staying at the Princeton over on Oak Lane."

The lobby of the Princeton Hotel, Ki soon discovered, was even shabbier than that of Lois's former residence, the Hotel Deluxe. The stairs that led to the upper stories were shakier. But the room was almost indistinguishable from the one he had been in at the Deluxe with Lois. It contained a wooden chair. A pitcher, cracked, and a basin, also cracked, sat on a scarred bureau that had one missing drawer. A brass bed with a mattress that sagged in the middle was against one wall. Someone, maybe Lois, had clipped a picture of Lily Langtry from Godey's Ladies Book and tacked it on the wall above the bed.

Ki stared at Lily's curvaceous figure as Lois proceeded to unbuckle his belt. Then she unbuttoned his jeans and pulled them and his underwear down around his knees.

"It should have been a soldier," she said coyly, caressing his shaft. "It always snaps so smartly to attention."

She proceeded then to put Ki's soldier through basic training. Her maneuvers brought first a sigh and then a groan from Ki's lips. He sat down on the edge of the bed and let Lois pull off his boots and then his clothes.

"Now that you're naked as a snake," she said with a dimpled smile, "we can get down to business."

And get down to business she promptly did to Ki's delight. She dropped to her knees in front of him and gripped his erection in one hot hand, studying it with a critical eye. Then she eagerly tasted it, her lips nibbling it, her tongue tickling it.

Ki put his hands, palms down, behind him on the bed and leaned back, prepared to enjoy her ministrations. Enjoy them he did as Lois's head bobbed up and down on his stone-stiff erection and her tongue laved him. He exulted in the satin-soft embrace of her lips and reveled in the fiery furnace of her mouth. He could feel a spasm shoot through his testicles; he could sense the explosion that was coming.

Lois released him. "Let me catch my breath," she murmured, wiping her lips with the back of her hand.

Ki groaned his disappointment at her sudden withdrawal, but his groan faded away as she once again took him into her mouth and began to suck with a passion and intensity the likes of which he could not recall ever having experienced before. He shifted position slightly and thrust himself deeper into her mouth.

She gagged and started to withdraw, but Ki clasped his

hands behind her head and held her in place, unwilling to let her go this time and thus lose the wild sensations she was stirring in him.

She was breathing heavily now and making wet sounds, a slurp, a gurgle, another slurp. As he rose from the bed and stood before her, they were still locked together in an erotic embrace.

His hands remained clasped behind her head as she adjusted her own body to his new stance and began again to bob her head back and forth as she sucked his shaft. He began to move his hips. Soon he was matching her rhythm. As her head moved back, so did his pelvis. As her head moved forward and her lips devoured inch after glistening inch of his shaft, so did his pelvis so that his rigid lance of flesh disappeared completely into her mouth and her lips were momentarily pressed against the curly pubic hair darkening his crotch.

They kept at it for another minute, and then it began. Ki could feel himself tightening, could feel himself getting ready to erupt. He braced himself, threw back his head, arched his neck, let out a cry of pure ecstasy. The dam of his passion burst, flooding the kneeling Lois's mouth and throat.

She hungrily devoured his seed, firmly gripping his bare thighs in both hands as she did so, her lips still tightly encircling Ki's rod. She kept at it until his hips stopped bucking and his hands fell away from the back of her head.

As he eased himself out of her mouth and sat down on the bed, she swallowed several times, bent forward, and began to lick his testicles.

He fell back on the bed, threw his arms out at his sides, closed his eyes, and gloried in what she was doing to him. Time no longer existed for him. Only Lois's tongue existed. Her tongue and his testicles. Her giving and his taking. He was lost in a world that had become one hot erotic delight, in a lusty sea in which he was happy to let himself drown.

"You fell asleep on me!" Lois told Ki some time later when he opened his eyes and looked up to find her sitting cross-legged on the bed and staring down at him.

"Sorry," he apologized. "You just about wore me out, Lois, and that's a fact. Besides which I was up before dawn this morning. I guess it all kind of finally caught up with me."

"I thought you were bored with me."

Ki reached up, pulled her down to him, and kissed her on the tip of her nose. "Bored with you. That's like saying I'd be bored if somebody handed me a million dollars."

"Oh, Ki, you're so cute, and you say the sweetest things!" Lois threw her arms around him and squeezed him so hard he could barely catch his breath.

But he did manage to ask, "What time is it?"

"Wait a minute. I'll find out. There's a clock in Counselor Hayes's office, which you can see from the window." Lois sprang up and went to the window. Peering out, she announced, "It's five minutes to nine." Turning from the window, she asked, "Why?"

Ki was already up and struggling hurriedly into his clothes. He pulled on his boots and gave Lois a farewell wave. "Be seeing you. Soon, I hope."

After leaving the room, he sprinted down the stairs and out of the hotel. He raced down the street and almost collided with the telegraph operator who was just leaving the General Mercantile, the key to its front door in his hand.

"Did I get an answer to my telegram?" he breathlessly asked the man.

"Yes, you did. Now get out of my way, young man. I have to lock up."

"Not before you give me my telegram." Ki hustled the

32

spluttering and protesting operator back into the store where the man, still spluttering and still protesting lit a lamp, rummaged through a pile of papers on his desk, and came up with a yellow sheet that he grudgingly handed to Ki.

Ki read the message, holding it close to the low-burning lamp, which was almost wickless.

CIRCLE STAR HERD ARRIVED LEASED LAND NINE DAYS AGO STOP LEFT NEXT DAY STOP PAID GRASS MONEY TO AGENCY STOP UNDERSIGNED KNOWS NOTHING OF DROVER BILLY MACKENZIE STOP

AMOS BUTLER
INDIAN AGENT

"I have to send another telegram," Ki told the man who was glaring at him, his lips pursed in a petulant pout. "Did you hear what I said?"

The telegraph operator grunted and grudgingly handed Ki a message form.

Ki quickly filled it out, paid the fee the man demanded, and stood over him as he tapped out the Morse code message to Tom Breyer in Dodge City.

"What time do you open up in the morning?" Ki asked when his message had been sent.

"Seven A.M. sharp. Now, if you don't mind, I'm going home to bed."

Ki pounded on the door. When he got no answer, he pounded on it again.

Finally, a sleepy female voice called out, "Who's't?"

"Lois, it's me. Ki. Let me in."

Several minutes later, a key turned in the lock, and the

door was opened by a yawning Lois who was wearing a gaudily flowered satin nightgown and bedroom slippers that sported pink pom poms.

"What do you want?" she whispered, blinking up at Ki.

He embraced her and whispered in her ear.

"*That's* what you want?" she asked, pretending shock.

He nodded. Grinned.

"Well, you came to the right place to get it. Come on in."

At seven o'clock the next morning, Ki was eating a huge breakfast of fried ham, fried potatoes, four scrambled eggs, bread, butter and coffee at Mrs. Pike's Plain and Fancy Eats restaurant across the street from the Princeton Hotel.

He thought about the night just ended as he devoured the food he had ordered and emptied his coffee cup for the second time that morning. It had been a night to remember. A night he wouldn't soon forget. It had left him sore in several strategic places. But also thoroughly satisfied. Lois was, he thought, the eighth wonder of the world. A woman of many talents, all of which she had displayed to him during the long hours of the now dead night.

"Dessert, sir?"

Ki looked up at the waiter who had appeared out of nowhere. "What do you have?"

The waiter said he had apple pie, cinnamon tarts, and vanilla sherbert.

Ki ordered one of each and another cup of coffee.

Just before eight o'clock, he entered the General Mercantile and asked the telegraph operator if there had been a reply to the message he had sent to Dodge City the night before.

The operator handed him a message form.

CIRCLE STAR HERD LONG OVERDUE STOP
NO WORD FROM BOB STATLER STOP NEED
CATTLE FOR EASTERN BUYERS STOP WHAT
IS WRONG STOP

TOM BREYER

Ki thrust the message into his pocket and left the store. He went to where his horse still stood in front of the Golden Calf saloon. He removed the nose bag from the animal, which he had gotten from the livery stable before he had gone to have his breakfast. He returned it to the stable boy, paid for the feed it had contained, and returned to his horse where he stepped into the saddle and rode out of town.

He reached the Circle Star ranch at mid-morning. He left his horse outside, not taking the time to put it in the barn, and went inside. He found Jessie in the kitchen planning menus with the cook.

She excused herself when she saw him and left the kitchen with him. In the great room, she looked expectantly at him.

"I wired Darlington," he informed her as he handed her the reply he had received from Amos Butler, the Indian agent.

When she had read it and looked up at him, he said, "I also got in touch with Tom Breyer at Dodge." He gave her Beyer's disturbing reply and watched her read it.

"Something's wrong," she said when she had finished reading Breyer's words.

"I agree. But what puzzles me is this. If Statler had run into trouble on the trail that delayed him I would have thought he would have notified Breyer of that fact. The buyers from the East aren't going to wait around forever for cattle. If they can't buy Circle Star stock, they'll buy somebody's else's. But Statler could have avoided that if he had simply sent word to Breyer that he would be arriving late. That would have been the way to hold on to the Circle Star's beef buyers."

"It may be that he didn't send word to Breyer because he couldn't do so," Jessie speculated. "It may be that he didn't get to Dodge because he couldn't get there for some reason."

Ki was conscious of Jessie's leaden tone of voice and also well aware of the worry that lay behind its colorlessness. "I could go north and see if I can find Statler and the herd," he volunteered.

Jessie crossed the room and sat down in a wing chair. She steepled her fingers and stared sightlessly at them. "I have a bad feeling about this, Ki."

So do I, he thought but he remained silent, waiting for her to go on.

"I know Bob Statler well. He has worked for Starbuck Enterprises for many years. He's dependable. So are the drovers he took with him. There's not a man among them who wouldn't have notified Breyer in Dodge, or me, if something had happened to prevent them from completing the drive in good order and within a reasonable amount of time.

"The fact that we, none of us, have heard from anyone concerning the whereabouts of the men and the cattle makes it seem as if they have just vanished. Which is patently impossible."

"Unless," Ki said, "somebody for some reason saw to it that they vanished."

Jessie rose and went to the window. She stood there for a long moment, staring out at the sun-filled world outside, saying nothing. Then, "Statler got the herd as far as the leased land on the Cheyenne and Arapaho reservation. We know that from Agent Butler's telegraph message. Whatever happened to him and his men, if indeed anything did, happened after they left for Dodge with the fattened cattle they picked up on the leased land."

She turned to face Ki. "How soon can you be ready to leave here?"

"I'm ready right now."

"I have a few things to take care of before we go. They shouldn't take long. I'll meet you outside in half an hour. We'll leave then."

★
Chapter 3

After nearly two full days of traveling by train, Jessie and Ki finally arrived at Wichita Falls, Texas, just south of the lone star state's northern border beyond which was Indian Territory.

Jessie now wore a gunbelt. From it hung the cordovan leather holster that contained her double action Colt .38, which was mounted on a sturdy .44 frame. It was a weapon she favored for the very practical reason that it had less recoil than heavier weapons. Although its rounds did not pack the punch of .44 slugs, she had always found that it served its purpose well and faithfully.

She also favored the gun for an unabashedly sentimental reason. It had been especially commissioned for her by her father from the Colt factory in Connecticut some years ago. She found it aesthetically pleasing, and she took pleasure in its slate-gray finish and grips of polished peachwood.

The Colt was not the only weapon she carried. In the pocket of her fringed buckskin jacket was a double barreled .38 caliber derringer, which had engraved on its ivory grips the star within a circle, the symbol of the Starbuck empire.

In Wichita Falls, Jessie and Ki rented saddle horses and a pack horse at the local livery stable. They bought provisions for the next leg of their journey and loaded them on the pack horse that, they had been assured by the stableman, was one which would "lead easy."

They left Wichita Falls in mid-afternoon on an overcast

day and forded the Red River that evening, traveling northeast as they headed for the one hundred and twenty thousand acres of land leased by Starbuck Enterprises from the Cheyenne and Arapaho Indians. The leased land was located twelve miles due west of Fort Reno and fifteen miles southwest of the town of Darlington.

They made camp that night in a shallow valley that offered a plentiful supply of both wood and water. Over their evening meal, which Ki cooked, there was conversation on many topics, but both Jessie and Ki seemed to be avoiding discussing the one topic that was at the forefront of both of their minds. Neither of them mentioned the herd and men that had left the leased land but had never arrived at Dodge City. Neither of them mentioned Billy MacKenzie, although they had visited the MacKenzie home before leaving on their journey in order to assure Billy's parents that they would let them know just as soon as they had any definite word on the whereabouts of their son.

Mrs. MacKenzie had been both grateful and tearful. Mr. MacKenzie, a hardbitten but softspoken man, had thanked them for "taking an interest" and had said he was sure things would "turn out all right." His voice, however, had not carried much conviction, and Mrs. MacKenzie must have noticed that fact because fresh tears spilled from her eyes when her husband had finished speaking.

After finishing their supper, Jessie carried their tin plates and cutlery down to the bank of the stream, which flowed close to where they had made camp to wash them. Meanwhile, Ki picketed their horses in a grove of quaking aspens that offered shelter from the strong wind that had begun to blow soon after darkness settled on the land.

Later, they both lay sleepless and silent, staring up at the multitude of stars that packed the sky and appeared close enough to reach up and touch.

From the aspens came the sound of a horse nickering. In

the distance, a wolf howled, howled again, and then fell silent.

They were on the trail early the next morning after a bracing breakfast of beans that had boiled all night on the banked fire and cups of Ki's coffee, which Jessie praised as "strong enough to stand a spoon straight up in."

They traveled past fences under construction and past stretches of land denuded of timber that had been cut to provide the posts for the fences, both signs of the presence of cattlemen and cattle companies on reservation land they had leased from the Indians.

"If I've got my bearings right," Jessie commented as they rode over a stretch of lush grassland, "this is part of the Solomon Brothers' lease. It runs east of here for several more miles."

Late that afternoon, as they rode along an unfinished length of fence, Ki was the first to spot the lone rider aboard a big bay up ahead of them. "Company's coming," he told Jessie.

She watched the man approach.

"Do you know him?" Ki asked.

"No. But then I haven't been up here since I took part in negotiating the lease for our land with Chief Howler of the Cheyenne and Chief No Blankets of the Arapaho. He's probably one of the men who ride for the Solomon brothers."

The man stood up in his stirrups, took off his hat, and waved a greeting. Jessie did the same. Only then did the man complete his journey toward them.

When he arrived, he was smiling. "My it is good to see a white woman out here in this godforsaken wilderness," he declared, his eyes on Jessie. "It's even better to see such a *pretty* white woman. I hope you don't mind me being so forward, ma'am. It's just that you took my breath clear away when I saw you, and I guess that's loosened up my tongue some."

"I'm Jessica Starbuck. This is my friend, Ki."

"How do, Miss Starbuck? You too, Ki. You're on your way to the Starbuck land, are you?"

"Yes, we are," Jessie answered.

"My name's Jim Hanson. I work for Mr. Chet Lancaster whose land it is you're on right at the moment."

"I thought we were still on Solomon Brothers' land," a surprised Jessie remarked.

"You would be were it not for the fact that the Solomon Brothers sublet half of their spread to Mr. Lancaster six months back."

Hanson gave Ki an appraising glance and then turned his attention to Jessie once again. "Why don't you two ride along with me? I'm ready to head back to our base camp, and it's in the direction you're going."

"We'd be glad to," Jessie said.

"I was just out here checking on our fence," Hanson volunteered as the trio headed east. "We got a lot of the post holes dug and some of the posts put in place, but the barbed wire we ordered, it's not yet arrived though Mr. Lancaster ordered it weeks ago. You got to keep an eye on your fences here on the reservation. Some of the Injuns cut the wire and pull up the posts about as fast as a man can put them in."

"Why is that?" Ki asked.

"Oh, just pure cussedness, I reckon. Only they say, the fence busters do, that we got no right to be on their land."

"But we pay for the privilege of grazing our cattle here," Jessie pointed out. "The Cheyenne and Arapaho tribal treasuries are enriched as a result of the arrangements we've made with the Indians."

"That's true enough as far as it goes," Hanson agreed, "but it seems like there's some in both tribes who think the land went way too cheap. Two cents an acre for grazing

41

rights is not enough, they claim. Then there's others who say flat out that no white cattlemen or women, like in your case, Miss Starbuck, ought to be let on Indian land in the first place or at any price. Between the two bunches, we've got our hands full."

"They've torn down your fences?" Ki inquired.

"That and worse," Hanson replied. "They're thieves, every manjack of them. They steal cattle, and if you catch them at it, they claim they're hungry. They say their beef ration hasn't showed up and their kids are cranky or some such thing. Cattlemen out here have lost a goodly number of animals to the miscreants, and they're not one bit happy about it."

"Mr. Hanson—"

"Call me Hanson, Miss Starbuck. No need to be formal. Now, what was it you were about to say?"

"I wanted to ask you if you by any chance know a man who works for me. His name is Bob Statler."

"No, ma'am, I don't know the name. He works on the land you leased?"

"No, he was in charge of bringing some stock up here from our ranch in Texas. He was to pick up some fattened cattle on the reservation and drive them on to Dodge. I know he left here for Dodge. I was going to ask you if you had seen him heading north from our range."

"No, I can't say as how I seen him. But then that doesn't mean a thing out here in the Territory. This is a mighty big country. Statler and his herd, they could have traveled north without a soul within ten, twenty miles laying an eye on them."

This is a mighty big country.

Hanson's words echoed in Jessie's mind. What he had said was certainly true. And, being true, it was going to make her task more difficult. Where did one begin to look for a herd of cattle and the men accompanying it in a land where distances were commonly measured not in scores but in hundreds of miles?

"You looking for this Statler fella, are you, Miss Starbuck?" Hanson asked.

Jessie, lost in thought, didn't hear his question.

It was Ki who answered it. "We are. As Miss Starbuck has said, we know that Statler left here and headed for Dodge. To the best of our knowledge, he and his herd never got there."

Jessie, pushing her disturbing thoughts aside, heard Hanson's next remark, which brought her no comfort.

"Maybe Statler ran into some Injun trouble."

"There has been trouble with the Indians?" Ki prompted when Hanson did not elaborate.

"Nothing serious. Not yet. A few shooting scrapes. No scalping that I've heard of. But there's talk. Hot talk it is too."

"Can you be more specific?" Jessie prodded.

"Sure, I can. There's some talk that the Cheyenne are itching to head back home. That would be the northern Cheyenne, of course. They don't much fancy it down this far south. They can't seem to get used to the climate. On top of that, there's hardly a buffalo to be found around here anymore. Amos Butler—"

"The Indian agent at the Darlington Agency," Ki said, recognizing the name.

"That's the fella," Hanson said, nodding. "Butler authorized a hunt this spring. A few weeks back, as a matter of fact. The Cheyenne found only two buffalo. Can you believe that? Just two? Why, these here plains used to be so chock full of buffalo you couldn't move without you ran into at least one of them and more likely all of his first and second cousins at the selfsame time."

"To get back to the Indian trouble you referred to, Hanson," Jessie said. "Have any drovers been bothered by the Indians?"

"Not that I know of. But all this talk, it's giving the people up on the border conniption fits. I was up in Dodge a month back on a supply run, and that's all you heard up there. Are the redskins going to jump the reservation? Are those heathen going on the warpath again? It had most folk as skittish as a colt that smells cougar stink riding in on the wind."

Jessie and Ki exchanged glances but neither of them said anything.

"That's our base camp yonder," Hanson announced, pointing to the fire glowing in the distance and the men who stood and sat around it. "Those few hundred head north of the camp are a part of our herd."

When they arrived at the cow camp and had dismounted, Hanson took Jessie by the arm and guided her around the fire to where a tall man with a lean face and leaner body stood cradling a cup of coffee in his work-worn hands.

"Howdy, boss," Hanson greeted the man. "It's my pleasure to introduce to you this here lady whose name is Jessica Starbuck. Miss Starbuck, this here's my boss, Chet Lancaster."

"How do you do, Mr. Lancaster? I've heard about you, but I didn't know we were neighbors until a little while ago."

"I'm happy to meet you, Miss Starbuck. I too have heard a great deal about you. All of it, I hasten to add, most complimentary. Very much so, as a matter of fact." Lancaster emptied his cup on the ground and then handed it to Hanson before shaking hands with Jessie.

"This is my friend, Ki," Jessie said and watched as the two men shook hands.

"We understand, Mr. Lancaster," Ki said, "that you've acquired a portion of the Solomon Brothers' grazing land."

"Yes, that's so. Which makes me a neighbor of your

44

friend, Miss Starbuck, as she has just pointed out to me. A pleasant situation, I call it."

"Boss, I'll be moseying on if that's all right with you."

Lancaster gave Hanson a nod, and Hanson moved away in what Jessie thought was a decidedly obsequious manner. This might be due, she thought, to Lancaster's rather imposing presence and bearing.

The cattleman was tall, and he had about him, Jessie thought, an air of quiet strength. There was, too, something about him that could, she thought, be cruel. It had been apparent in the curtly dismissive nod he had just given Hanson. It could be sensed as well in the faintly contemptuous way he had of speaking, as if those he spoke to were beneath him.

His deeply set eyes were blue ice. His blond hair was curly and hid his ears and half of his broad forehead. He wore typical trail clothes, but no one would ever mistake him for a common cowboy. There was something almost imperial in his bearing.

Imperial. Cruel. Contemptuous. The words, Jessie decided, weren't unfairly applied to Chet Lancaster. On the contrary, they fit him like a tight glove in her judgment.

"I take it you've only recently arrived on the reservation," he remarked.

"How did you know that?" Ki asked him.

Lancaster pointed to the pack horse Ki had been trailing when they arrived.

"You're right," Jessie said.

"Have you come to check on your operation, Miss Starbuck?"

"No. Ki and I have come here to try to track down a herd and the men who were driving it to Dodge."

Lancaster's eyebrows rose. "You've lost a herd and its drovers? Or are you telling me that your drovers have made off with the herd?"

"I'm telling you neither," Jessie said with an edge to her

voice, not liking the mocking tone Lancaster had just used. Stop it, she told herself. He was just trying to make a joke. "We've been told that Bob Statler, he was the drive's trail boss, arrived on the range we lease here and then moved on with some stock intended for sale in Dodge. We've also been told that he and his herd have not arrived in Dodge although they were due there days ago."

"Very mysterious but not altogether unheard of," Lancaster commented. "Trail drives, as you must know, are subject to all sorts of misadventures."

"You believe the men have had a misadventure?" Ki asked.

"I didn't say that. How could I say that? I have no knowledge of your Mr. Statler and his crew. No, that is not quite true. I did meet Mr. Statler once but quite briefly."

"When was that?" Jessie asked.

"Let me see. About two weeks ago. I can't be absolutely sure of the date but two weeks is probably pretty close to correct."

"Where did you meet him?" Ki interjected.

"On the land you lease east of here. I was traveling over it on my way to the Darlington Agency to pay my grass money and stopped to visit with your Circle Star hands. Pleasant enough lot. As was Mr. Statler."

"Was he in good health, would you say, when you met him?" Jessie asked.

"Yes, he was or appeared to me to be. As did all your trail hands."

"Was there a young boy with them?" Jessie inquired. "A boy of fifteen? Hair as blond and eyes as blue as yours?"

Lancaster pondered the question a moment. "I believe there was such a youngster present at the time. Yes, I'm sure there was. I remember thinking that he was trying very hard to seem quite grown up. He used, as I recall some rather strong and colorful language when he scalded his tongue with some hot coffee." Lancaster laughed. "He

46

was a mere stripling but trying most valiantly to be a man among men."

"Did you see Statler or any of his men after that initial meeting?" Ki asked.

Lancaster shook his head. "No. When I returned across the Circle Star range, I was told by one of your men, Miss Starbuck, that Statler had headed north with some cattle."

"It's a puzzling and disturbing situation," Jessie commented thoughtfully.

"Disturbing, yes," Lancaster ventured. "Puzzling, no."

Ki frowned. "What do you mean?"

"It's possible, you know, that your trail boss might have decided to confiscate your cattle. Take them to a railhead other than Dodge. Sell them there and pocket the money."

"Bob Statler would never do a thing like that," Jessie insisted somewhat heatedly.

"I'm not saying he did. I'm merely suggesting that there are many possible explanations for the failure of your cattle to arrive at their destination. Are you quite sure they never did arrive?"

"The broker we do business with in Dodge said the herd had not arrived."

"And you believe him?"

"I believe him."

"Well, Miss Starbuck, I can only sympathize with your plight and wish you luck in locating your lost herd. If there is anything I can do to help, I shall be only too glad to do so. My men and other resources are at your command should you find you have need of them."

"Thank you, Mr. Lancaster," Jessie said, somewhat taken aback by the cattleman's generous offer. And also somewhat ashamed of her earlier harsh judgment of him. "That's a very kind and thoughtful offer."

"Are you in a hurry to reach your leased land?" Lancaster asked, changing the subject.

"Why do you ask?"

"You and Ki both look a little tired if you don't mind my saying so. I was about to offer you the hospitality of my camp for the night, rude as that hospitality may prove to be."

"Again I have to thank you for your kindness and generosity. To tell you the truth, I am feeling a bit bushed. What about you, Ki?"

"It will be getting dark soon. I'd be pleased to accept Mr. Lancaster's offer to spend the night here."

"Then the matter is decided," Lancaster declared. "Supper will be ready shortly. Now, if you'll both excuse me, I'll find Hanson and have him put up your horses for the night. Both of you make yourselves at home."

When Lancaster had gone, Ki turned to Jessie and remarked, "He's a real smooth one, isn't he? Smooth as glass, I'd say, but a lot harder to see through."

Jessie gave him an inquisitive glance.

"He seems straightforward enough," Ki added. "He certainly is generous."

"But . . ." Jessie prompted. Knowing Ki as well as she did, she was aware that something was bothering him. Something lay beyond his apparently positive evaluation of Lancaster.

"But I have the strong feeling that there's more to that man than meets the eye."

Jessie was about to question Ki, to ask him what exactly he meant by his remark, but before she could do so, there was a sudden noisy commotion at the far end of the camp.

She turned to see what was causing it and saw at first only a cloud of dust and several of Lancaster's men running in all directions.

"Indians," Ki said.

Jessie saw no Indians. But, a moment later, several appeared from out of the rising dust they had stirred up. The wind had blown the dust ahead of them, thus effectively, but only momentarily, hiding them from sight.

48

There were five of them, all Cheyenne. The one who seemed to be their leader mockingly raised both of his hands when one of Lancaster's men, a red-bearded cowboy, raised a six-gun and aimed it at him.

"It is the white way," the Indian said, his lips curling in an unmistakable sneer. "Go first for gun. You want to kill me and my men?"

The question had been addressed to the red-bearded cowboy with the gun who looked away, apparently unable to meet the Indian's piercing gaze.

"Put the weapon away, Tolliver," Lancaster said as he emerged from a a grove of trees with Hanson right behind him.

Tolliver hesitated, and then succumbing to Lancaster's glare that was as piercing as the look in the Cheyenne's eye, he holstered his gun and stepped back as if in retreat before the visitors.

"You're Big Buffalo," Lancaster said, taking up a position a few yards in front of the Indians who had just taunted the cowboy.

"Brave Buffalo," the Cheyenne corrected.

"I beg your pardon, Brave Buffalo. What brings you here to my camp?"

"Him."

"Me?" Hanson squeaked nervously, jabbing an index finger against his chest.

"He is a thief," Brave Buffalo intoned.

His words were followed by guttural grunts from the four men accompanying him.

Jessie looked from the Cheyenne to Hanson who stood shaking his head in mute denial of the Indian's accusation. She looked back at Brave Buffalo who sat his horse with a kind of dignity and grace that few white horsemen she had ever seen possessed.

He's handsome, she found herself thinking. Strong. Virile. Very much in control of himself and his men.

"You steal Cheyenne ponies," Brave Buffalo declared, his eyes on Hanson. "Four ponies you stole yesterday from Cheyenne when the sun was down and night had come. You stole them from Has Horses." Brave Buffalo indicated the Indian on his left.

"Is true," Has Horses said flatly. "I see you steal ponies. My woman see you. My daughter, she see you."

"Mr. Lancaster, that's not true what they're accusing me of!" Hanson protested, clutching his employer's sleeve.

Lancaster shook him off.

"I never stole no ponies from him or any other Indian. I swear I didn't!"

"You heard my man," Lancaster said, addressing Brave Buffalo. "It is the word of Has Horses against that of Jim Hanson here. It seems we've reached a standoff."

"Give him to us," Brave Buffalo demanded.

"*Give* him to you?" an incredulous Lancaster said. He gave a short snort of derisive laughter. "I will not give him to you. I will instead demand that you leave this camp and leave here now or I will not be responsible for any actions taken against you by my men."

"Hanson stole Cheyenne ponies," Brave Buffalo said, repeating his accusation. "Give him to us."

"Look," Lancaster said. "The thing for you to do in a situation like this is to take Hanson to court in Kansas. In Dodge City or Lawrence. That's the way to resolve this dispute. I know you Indians have taken white men who you claimed were horse thieves to court. If you're so sure of your facts, go to court with them."

"Agent Butler say he have no money to pay to send Has Horses and his woman and his daughter to court in Kansas. Has Horses has no money to go to Kansas with his woman and daughter to get justice. We settle this our way. Cheyenne way. Give Hanson to us."

Jessie stiffened as Lancaster gave an almost impercepti-ble nod and all of his men drew their guns.

Lancaster, speaking in a low tone, said, "I know you by sight and reputation, Brave Buffalo. I know you are the top man in the Cheyenne Dog Soldier Society. I also know that you have been stealing cattle from me and other people who have leased your land to graze their stock on, like Miss Starbuck here."

Brave Buffalo's eyes rested on Jessie and remained there as Lancaster continued. "You're a bad Indian, Brave Buffalo. I don't want bad Indians around me and my men, not to mention my cattle. Move out now or . . ." Lancaster didn't complete his sentence.

Has Horses whispered something to Brave Buffalo who nodded and said to Lancaster, "You will not give us horse thief Hanson. Give us beef instead. One beef for each pony Hanson stole from Has Horses."

Without a moment's hesitation, Lancaster barked, "No."

Jessie moved to his side. "Why not give them four head of cattle? If what Brave Buffalo says is true, it's a small price to pay to maintain the peace. All of us have to learn to live together here on the reservation."

"You heard what Hanson said, Miss Starbuck. He denies this savage's charge. What's more, I've already lost cows to these scavengers. I don't intend to lose any more, nor do I intend to be intimidated by men who, thieves themselves, are all too ready and eager to accuse other men of the same crime with no proof to support their claim."

Jessie tried again to persuade Lancaster to change his mind and give beef to the Cheyenne, but she failed to do so.

"I told you once and I'm telling you again," Lancaster said to Brave Buffalo and the men with him. "Get off my land."

"Your land?" Brave Buffalo shot back.

"I lease it, and I pay grass money to your tribe's treasury twice a year for the privilege. Yes, it damn well is *my* land at the moment."

Has Horses leaned toward Brave Buffalo and spoke softly to him.

Again Brave Buffalo nodded. He gave a hand signal, and the Indians with him turned their horses and rode back the way they had come without another word.

"Well, it looks like that's that," a satisfied Lancaster commented, watching the retreating Indians who were heading toward the cattle on their bed-ground in the distance.

"You sure made short work of them heathen, boss," Hanson crowed happily. "You didn't give an inch. They backed right off with their tails tucked between their legs. Oh, my, but wasn't that a pretty sight to see!"

"What is the Dog Soldier Society you mentioned?" Ki asked Lancaster.

"It's one of the Cheyenne warrior societies. The Dog Soldiers fancy themselves to be the champions of the way things were in the old days when the Cheyenne hunted and lived on the northern plains. The fact is that they are the source of a whole passel of problems. Which come from the fact that the old ways are deader than a doornail, but they simply won't face up to that fact. They're always at loggerheads with the half-bloods and those smart Indians who take on the white man's way."

"I'll go see to our guests' horses, boss," Hanson said and left.

"If you and Ki will excuse me, Miss Starbuck," Lancaster said, "I have some things I want to tend to before we all sit down to supper."

"Mr. Lancaster," Jessie said before he could leave.

"Yes?"

"I think you've got yourself a problem."

Before Lancaster could ask her what she meant, one of his hands, a hatless man wearing a black bandanna around his head as a sweatband, shouted, "Boss, those Indians are stealing some of our stock!"

★

Chapter 4

"Stop those thieving savages!" Lancaster bellowed at the top of his voice when he saw what Jessie had first noticed. Brave Buffalo and his companions were trying to cut four head of cattle out of the herd.

"Shoot them if you have to!" Lancaster roared, his face reddening with rage.

"Let's go get 'em boys!" Hanson cried.

Lancaster's men went running for their horses. They drew their guns and, once mounted, went racing toward the herd and the Indians in the distance.

Shots sounded. A flurry of them.

Ki counted a total of six. "They're going to stampede that herd," he told Jessie, "if they don't stop the ruckus they're raising."

"If they do that, they'll certainly have their hands full. They might lose a lot more than four head if a full-blown stampede starts."

"It's started," Ki declared grimly.

The herd had begun to move like a horned tidal wave. They moved slowly at first, a number of them clumsily rising from where they had been lying to join the others that were beginning to flee from the sharp sound of gun-fire.

"Can I borrow your horse?" Ki asked Jessie.

"Yes, but what—"

Jessie didn't finish her question because Ki was racing

away from her toward the spot where Hanson had taken their horses, and he was already out of earshot. She watched him leap into the saddle of her horse and go riding at a gallop after Lancaster's men.

When she saw Ki free the length of coiled rope that hung from her saddle horn, she realized why he had wanted to use her horse rather than his own; he had no rope among the gear on his own mount.

She became aware that Lancaster was no longer at her side. She turned her head and saw him riding, bent low over his horse's neck, as he headed toward his herd, which was moving faster now, mindlessly following the three steers that were leading the stampede. He's going to try to head them off, she thought, silently wishing him luck.

Brave Buffalo was riding away from the herd as he and his men drove the four head of cattle they had managed to cut from the rest of the herd. Swirling dust swallowed him, his men, and the cattle they had just taken. When the dust subsided, they were nowhere in sight.

Jessie ran to where Ki's horse stood idly browsing. Once in the saddle, she moved out, intending to do what she could to help stop the stampede. She knew from bitter experience that a number of the cows might be killed if they went over the cliffs or broke their legs and had to be shot.

Ki rode as fast as he could, blinking away the dust that seemed to be everywhere as best he could. But some got in his eyes, temporarily blinding him. Some also got in his throat, almost choking him.

"Hell's boiling over, boys!" a Lancaster rider yelled from somewhere behind him. *"Hold the herd!"*

The bawling cattle were rampaging now, an insanely surging sea of flesh, and the Lancaster men, belatedly realizing that it had been a mistake to fire their guns, had put them away. But it was a lesson learned too late to stop the herd that was on a headlong and potentially dangerous dash to nowhere.

When Ki reached the herd, he rode along its right flank, dodging other riders, until he was almost at the front of the mass of bodies. He kept up his horse-killing pace, his ears ringing as a result of the loud clatter and clash of horns as the animals collided with one another.

He shifted Jessie's rope to his left and and used it to lash the steers nearest to him. He succeeded in turning back two of the animals and slowing down several others. But his efforts were not enough to halt the rampage. He realized something was different now. What? At first, he wasn't sure. Then it came to him. The cattle, which had earlier been so loudly bawling, were now ominously silent as they plunged mindlessly ahead.

Ki, as he rode close to the packed mass of cattle, was grazed on the thigh by a steer's horn. As he involuntarily loosened his hold on his reins because of the pain that shot through his leg, his horse tried to bolt, but he fought successfully to keep control of it.

Other riders tried frantically to halt the herd, but all were unsuccessful. They, like the cattle, were silent as they went about their desperate task, their expressions grim.

Out of the corner of his eye, Ki saw Lancaster riding toward the herd. The man was lashing his mount with his reins, first one side, then the other.

Ki continued striking the nearest steers with Jessie's rope, but his actions seemed to have little or no effect on them.

He saw Lancaster loom up ahead of him. As the cattleman tried to head off the herd, his horse was gored by a steer's horn. It shied, lost its balance, and went down, throwing its rider to the ground.

Ki changed course and rode as fast as he could. He knew that if he didn't reach Lancaster in time the man was sure to be trampled to death by the onrushing herd.

When a steer suddenly and unexpectedly veered away from the main mass of racing cattle and into his path, Ki was forced to swerve sharply to avoid a potentially deadly collision. He managed to avoid the animal, but he had lost precious seconds. Up ahead of him, Lancaster was trying hard to get to his feet, but his right foot was caught beneath the body of his horse, which had been crushed to death by the stampeding steers.

When he finally reached Lancaster, he slid out of the saddle, bent down, and put his shoulder against the spine of Lancaster's dead horse. "Help me!" Ki ordered the cattleman.

Lancaster, his foot still pinned beneath the body of his horse, bent over and, together with Ki, fought to move the corpse off his foot. Their combined efforts were enough to move the body an inch. That inch turned out to be just enough. Lancaster managed to pull his foot free.

"Thanks," the pale cattleman said to Ki. "I thought I was a goner for sure until you showed up."

Ki sprang into the saddle and went after the herd, which was far ahead of him now.

But then it suddenly changed course for no apparent reason and headed back toward Ki. He continued to ride toward it. Then, at the last possible moment, he swerved to the side, turned his horse, and was once again riding on the herd's flank. He lashed out with his rope at one of the three lead steers. He struck a second time. To no effect.

A steer racing behind the lead animals suddenly tossed its head. It caught Ki's rope on its right horn and tore it out of his hand.

Ki cursed and rode on, his boots straining against his stirrups. His eyes stung from the gritty dust, and his throat felt like the floor of a desert.

Without slowing his horse, he freed his feet from his stirrups. Judging the movements of his mount, he got one leg under him and then, in one deft but dangerous move, stood up in his saddle. He maintained that postion for only an instant before leaping onto the back of one of the racing steers.

He landed with a bone-jarring *thunk* and seized handfuls of hide to keep himself from falling to his death under the pounding hooves of the tightly packed herd. Then he managed to get to his knees. A moment later, he was up on his feet atop the steer swaying precariously. He held his position for only a brief moment before throwing himself forward. He flew through the air for a distance of no more than two feet. This time he landed on the back of one of the three lead steers.

Holding tightly to the animal's long horn with his left hand, he drew from the sheath fastened to his belt the knife he carried.

Leaning forward and looking down, he deftly slashed twice with his knife. Then, without wasting a moment, he crawled on his hands and knees onto the back of the animal that was in the lead on the left of the steer he had just cut. Once there, he slashed that animal as he had the first.

Through the dust he was just barely able to see Jessie who had apparently taken command of the men in Lancaster's absence. As he crawled over to the third lead steer's back, he heard her shout orders to the men riding with her. As he cut the third steer in the same manner as he had the first two, he heard two shots fired. He saw a steer on the left flank of the herd go down and the ones behind it stumble and fall over its body. He turned his head and saw the same thing happen on the herd's opposite flank. He also saw Jessie deploy the men in such a way that they were performing a pincer movement, which was effectively blocking the headlong flight of the herd and rapidly slowing it down.

Their efforts, together with his own, finally brought the herd to a halt. As the beeves began to mill, Ki watched for his chance and then leaped from the back of the bloody-faced steer he had been holding onto so tightly. He hit the ground running. When he was safely away from the now aimlessly milling herd, he stopped to catch his breath.

"Are you all right?" Jessie called out as she rode up to him, an anxious expression on her face.

Ki, his throat too dry to speak, could only nod.

"When I saw you on the backs of those animals, I wanted to shut my eyes. I was sure you were going to fall and be crushed to death."

Ki coughed.

"What did you do to those beeves?" an irate Hanson bellowed at Ki as he rode up. "You've blinded them!"

Ki shook his head. He swallowed hard several times and them managed to croak, "You're wrong."

"I'm not wrong!" Hanson insisted. "Look at them! Their eyes are all bloody."

Ki opened his mouth to speak but could only gag on the dust that practically filled it.

Jessie handed him her canteen.

He drank from it and then, addressing Hanson, said, "I cut the muscles in the eyelids of those three lead steers, not their eyes. They'll be blind temporarily, but their eyelids will heal. They'll soon be able to see again. I had to do it. I couldn't stop the stampede leaders any other way. The only harm done is those three steers will have droopy eyelids for the rest of their lives, but I don't imagine Kansas beef buyers will mind that much."

"Where'd you ever learn a trick like that?" a mollified and obviously impressed Hanson asked.

"We had some rustlers running rampant on the Circle Star ranch down in Texas not long ago," Ki answered. "It was a trick they used. That's how they steal calves that aren't yet weaned. They cut their eyelids so they can't find their mothers. By the time their eyelids are healed, they're weaned, and the rustlers go ahead and slap their brands on them."

"Here comes the boss," one of the cowhands yelled.

Jessie turned and saw Lancaster riding up to them. The cattleman was seated behind another rider, and when they arrived both men dismounted.

"Is everything under control?" Lancaster asked, surveying the area.

"Pretty much so," Hanson answered. "The herd's in a mill, and it don't look like they're fixing to run again. We had to shoot a couple head to stop 'em, but most of the stopping was done by Ki here."

Lancaster directed a questioning gaze on Hanson who quickly explained what Ki had done to the lead steers to blind them temporarily and thus stop them.

Lancaster offered his hand, and Ki shook it. "I thank you, Ki. I'm in your debt. Yours too, Miss Starbuck. I saw you riding with my men, and I must say I never saw anyone, man or woman, make such smart moves and make them at the right moment as you just did."

"We were glad to be of help," Jessie said. Ki nodded his agreement with her.

"Let's go back to the camp," Lancaster suggested. "Now that things appear to have settled down we can take time out to eat some supper."

Early the next morning, Jessie and Ki made ready to leave Lancaster's cow camp.

"If there's ever anything I can do to repay you two for the good you did me yesterday," Lancaster told them as they climbed into their saddles, "you just give a holler, and I'll be sure to come running."

"We thank you for your hospitality," Jessie said. "That beef stew your cook prepared last night was the best I've ever tasted."

"I agree," Ki said. "In fact, I must confess that I've suggested to Jessie that she make the man an offer he can't refuse in order to get him to cook for the Circle Star hands."

"Matt's worth his weight in the proverbial gold," Lancaster said with a smile. "I don't think you'll be able to woo him away from me no matter how much money you might offer him. We've been together for years, Matt and I."

"I was only joking," Ki hastened to explain.

"I know you were. Well, good luck to you both. I hope we meet again. It's been a pleasure this time, I assure you."

Later that day, as Jessie and Ki rode northeast onto the land leased by Starbuck Enterprises, Ki said, "I thought those Lancaster men were going to blow Brave Buffalo and his friends to kingdom come when they stole those four steers."

"I thought so too. I'm glad they didn't. Hotheads like that nearly always cause more trouble than they're worth. The stampede they caused is a prime example of what I mean."

"Did you believe Brave Buffalo?"

"You mean did I believe his accusation that Jim Hanson stole four ponies from Has Horses?"

"Yes."

"I'm not sure whether I did or not. I think I believed him. I don't know why he would lie about a thing like that."

"Maybe he made up that story out of whole cloth to justify his subsequent taking of those steers from Lancaster's herd."

"I don't think that's true, Ki. Why would he go to all that trouble when he could have waited for nightfall and made off with the steers with, quite possibly, no one ever being the wiser?"

"Riders coming this way."

Jessie watched the three men as they galloped down

from a hummock to the north. "That's Joe Howard and two of his men. He leases land to the north of our range. He's been here longer than anyone else I know."

"Jessie!" Howard cried when he rode up and recognized her. "How nice to see you. And who is this?"

"A friend of mine, Joe. May I present Ki. Ki, Joe Howard."

The two men shook hands, and then Howard introduced the two men accomanying him.

"What are you doing off your range, Joe?" Jessie asked.

"Some of our stock has drifted. We're on the scout to round up any we find bearing my hayhook brand and take them on home where they belong. I'm sorry they've strayed onto your range, Jessie. My men will just have to keep a keener eye on our beeves."

"It's no problem, Joe."

"We'll ride along with you two if that's allright since we all seem to be heading the same way."

"Fine."

"What brings you up here, Jessie? I don't think I've seen you on the reservation for at least two years. Not since we all first negotiated our leases with the Indians."

"Bob Statler drove a herd up here. He was supposed to leave it here to graze and take some cattle that were ready for market up to Dodge City. I've lost track of him."

"Lost track of him?"

"Yes. I've had word that he did reach here—"

"I know for a fact he did. I saw him. He was heading north with some of your Circle Star cattle. When we met, he told me he was on his way to Dodge."

"As far as I can determine, Joe, he never got there, and frankly, I'm worried. Ki and I came up here to see if we can track him down."

"Where were you when you saw Mr. Statler?" Ki asked Howard. "Do you happen to recall?"

"Where was I? I was . . . I remember now. Statler and I

met east of here where my range abuts the Starbuck range. About five or so miles short of my boundary line. We rode north together for awhile. Talked over old times, the way you do. I was out with one of my men then, same as I'm out with these two boys now, hunting strays. Cattle do have an annoying tendency to wander, don't they? Anyway, I had to leave Statler behind because I wanted to move faster than his herd would let him. So we parted company. After we found our strays about nine miles north of where we met Statler and started back down south, we didn't run into him again. He must have left the Western Trail at some point and gone north by a different route."

"Maybe they ran into some trouble with the Indians," Jessie mused.

"What makes you say a thing like that?" Howard asked.

"We spent last night at Chet Lancaster's cow camp," Jessie replied. "One of his men indicated to us that there may be trouble brewing with the Cheyenne Indians. Do you think they could have had anything to do with Bob's mysterious disappearance?"

Howard shook his head. "That Indian trouble talk is mostly just that—talk. Every time an Indian speaks up for his rights, five nervous whites jump into bed, pull the covers over their heads, and start screaming about Indian trouble. Pay it no mind, Jessie. That's my advice."

"I was rather surprised to learn that Lancaster has taken over part of the Solomon Brothers' lease," Jessie said.

"Oh, Lancaster has been a very busy boy indeed," Howard declared. "He's ambitious, Lancaster is. Has ideas about becoming a cattle baron, if you ask me."

"Why did Solomon Brothers sublet to him?"

"They had to. They'd lost a lot of cattle. To Indians, they said. Lancaster claimed he was doing a favor taking over half of the land they lease from the two tribes. Helping them out of a hole is what he claimed he was doing. Which was true, looked at one way. Looked at another way, you could say he was taking advantage of their misfortune. They lost a lot of money, thanks to thieving redskins."

"What do the Indians do with the beef they steal?" Ki asked Howard.

"Eat it. It's do that or starve. The government doesn't deliver beef to the reservation regularly as they are supposed to do. Often, what they buy from beef contractors, is poor and sometimes sickly stuff. All bones and sinew. Hardly any meat on the critters at all. So the redskins steal steers whenever they need to keep body and soul together. You can't blame them in a way. It's sure enough no fun to have to sit around and watch your wife and offspring starve."

"Cheyenne Dog Soldiers ran off four steers from Lancaster's herd," Jessie said. "But they did that, I gather, because Lancaster wouldn't turn one of his men over to them. A man Brave Buffalo accused of stealing four Indian ponies from another Indian named Has Horses."

"That's the way of things out here these days," Howard remarked with a sigh. "The whites steal Indian horses to sell over the border in Kansas, and the Indians steal our beef to keep from starving to death."

"Sounds to me," Ki interjected, "like there's bound to be trouble sooner or later between the whites and the Indians with all this going on."

"There won't be," Howard said, "if people like us keep a tight rein on their men and if the government gets itself straightened out so that it can properly feed the Indians it has forcibly taken under its bureaucratic wing."

Howard cleared his throat and continued, "Have you run into any of the shysters out here on the reservation who claim to be leasing land without a piece of paper to prove it?"

"No," Jessie said. "There are such men?"

"There sure are. Thieves is what they are. They drive

cattle up here from Texas and let them graze on Indian land without paying one red cent into the tribal treasuries. They also, some of them, steal Indian ponies to make a bad matter worse. Then they drive what they steal up north along with their cattle and sell them there. But you've got enough troubles of your own without me harping on such stuff. What do you intend to do about your missing men and cattle, Jessie?"

"We intend to make inquiries about them. See what we can find out about their movements—anything at all that might help us locate them."

"Boss," said the rider on Howard's right. "There's our strays. Yonder."

"I see them. Let's go get them, boys. Nice seeing you again, Jessie. Nice meeting you, Ki. I hope you have good luck in your hunt for Statler and his herd."

As Jessie and Ki rode on without Howard and his men, they passed a small detachment of cavalry traveling in the opposite direction. The troopers were too far away to greet in passing but not too far away for Jessie to notice that the lieutenant leading the detachment seemed to be an attractive young man. But the sun was in her eyes, so she couldn't be sure her appraisal of him was accurate.

They had not gone far when they heard the sudden sound of angry voices coming from behind them. They turned and saw the lieutenant who had been leading the troopers engaged in a heated conversation with Joe Howard.

"It looks like those two are about to come to blows over something or other," Ki observed.

"They're certainly going at it toe-to-toe," Jessie commented as she watched the continuing confrontation between the two men, both of whom had dismounted and were angrily arguing, with only inches separating them from one another.

"Maybe Howard could use our help," Ki suggested.

"Let's go and find out."

They turned their horses and rode back toward the men who were still confronting one another. As they came closer to them, an occasional angry word or phrase could be heard drifting on the balmy breeze that was blowing across the plain.

Howard: ". . . not a single damned one . . ."

The lieutenant: ". . . twenty head . . ."

Howard: ". . . no . . ."

The lieutenant: ". . . yes . . ."

"What seems to be the problem, Joe?" Jessie asked as she and Ki rode up to the group and drew rein.

The lieutenant—he *was* attractive, Jessie saw for sure now that she was quite close to him—gave her a hostile look.

"This is Miss Jessica Starbuck," Howard said to the officer. "She's a friend of mine. Jessie, this is Lieutenant David Stowe. Now then, Lieutenant, I'd like to point out to you that with her and her friend, Ki, here, our two sides are almost evenly matched. There's five of us and seven of you."

Howard glanced at Jessie. "I shouldn't have said that. This is not your fight. You and Ki had best move on before the shooting starts."

Ki said, "Jessie's not one to run from a fight. Neither am I."

"There is no fight brewing here, as you put it, sir," Lieutenant Stowe stated rather stiffly in response to Ki's remarks. "We are simply in the process of conducting government business, and I would be obliged if you and your lady friend would kindly not interfere in a matter that does not concern you."

"Oh, but it does concern us," Jessie said with exaggerated sweetness as she smiled forthrightly at Lieutenant Stowe. "Mr. Howard is a friend, and we could not possibly stand idly by if he is in trouble and in need of our help."

"Ha!" snorted Howard, obviously pleased with the turn of events as he stared menacingly at Lieutenant Stowe.

Apparently deciding to ignore Jessie and Ki, Stowe turned his attention back to Howard. "Mr. Howard, you know you haven't got a leg to stand on in this matter. The government has the right to requisition beef from any herd it chooses. This time, it's your herd that's been chosen."

"You'll not take one of those beeves from me without a knockdown, drag-out fight," Howard announced.

"I have here a requisition. It has been signed by Major Lane, commandant of the Fourth Cavalry at Fort Reno." Stowe removed a piece of paper from his tunic pocket and waved it in front of Howard's face.

Howard promptly snapped it away. "You took ten head of mine last month, Lieutenant. You took five the month before. I've not gotten a dime in payment for any of them from the United States government, and if you ask me, I don't believe I'm ever likely to be paid for them."

"You know very well the bureaucracy in Washington moves slowly," Stowe pointed out. "The payments may be slow in coming, but you will receive them. I assure you of that."

"You're qualified to speak for the government, are you, Lieutenant?" Howard's tone reeked of sarcasm.

"What's all this about taking your stock?" Jessie asked him.

"The government's monthly beef ration hasn't arrived on the reservation according to Stowe," Howard angrily explained. "Again," he added bitterly. "So they send their tin soldiers out here to take beef from private individuals like us. But we never get paid for them, fancy requisitions signed by fancy commanding officers at Fort Reno notwithstanding."

"That doesn't seem fair," Ki commented. "The government ought to be willing to pay for what they confiscate."

"I don't like that word, sir," Stowe told him sternly.

"What word?" Ki asked.

"Confiscate. I prefer requisition."

"You can prefer till the cows come home," Howard bellowed. "But you aren't taking any more of my cattle without paying cash on the barrelhead for them. You got that, Lieutenant? Those are my terms. Take them or leave them."

"Now, see here—" Stowe began.

But Howard interrupted him. "Go farther west to Chet Lancaster's range. Confiscate—*requisition*—some of his steers and leave mine alone. How come you never take any of his cattle to feed all those hungry Indians the government's got over at the Darlington Agency? Why is that, Lieutenant?"

"Doesn't the government ever take any of Lancaster's stock?" Jessie asked.

"Never, not a single one," Howard replied.

She turned to Stowe and said. "That doesn't seem a bit fair to me, does it to you, Lieutenant?"

"Miss . . . Starbuck, is it? I don't write the orders or pass judgment on them. I only carry them out as my duty requires me to do."

"That Indian agent . . . Amos Butler," Howard muttered under his breath. "I'll wager ten to one he has a hand in all this somewhere. I reckon he sees to it that Lancaster's cattle are left alone. Either he does or that sissy assistant of his does."

"Agent Amos Butler and Assistant Agent Mark Demming," declared Stowe somewhat pompously, "merely ask the army, as an instrument of the federal government, to provide the agency with meat when it is needed. That is what we are here today to do."

"Then do it!" Howard snarled. "But do it with somebody else's beef."

"Be reasonable, Mr. Howard," Stowe pleaded.

"I *am* being reasonable!"

"Sergeant Breen!" a clearly annoyed Stowe snapped.

"Sir?" the sergeant behind him responded.

"Put Mr. Howard and his men under guard. Detail the remainder of the men to cut twenty head out of this bunch of cattle and start driving them to the Darlington Agency."

Sergeant Breen dismounted and drew his Army Colt. Brandishing it as he stepped in front of Lieutenant Stowe, he ordered, "Back off boys and let the army do the job it came out here to do."

Behind Breen and Stowe, the remaining soldiers rode toward the small herd of strays that were contentedly grazing not far away.

"No!" Howard roared and lunged for the sergeant.

Breen stepped nimbly out of the way, swung his gun, and struck Howard on the side of the head with its barrel.

Blood flooded through the suddenly broken skin on Howard's temple as he fell stunned to the ground as a result of the unexpected blow.

Ki sprang forward. With his right hand, he knocked the Colt from Sergeant Breen's hand. His left forearm went around the startled sergeant's neck. He spun around, bent over, and threw the sergeant over his shoulder. Before the downed man could make a move, Ki put a booted foot on his neck, pressing the side of his face into the ground. He picked up the gun Breen had dropped and, turning to face the troopers, said, "Now, which one of you soldier boys wants to try to take me?"

"Don't anybody try to or he'll answer to me," Jessie said sharply as she drew her gun and aimed it directly at Lieutenant Stowe.

★
Chapter 5

"Ki, let the sergeant up," Jessie said. When Ki had done so, she continued, addressing Lieutenant Stowe, "Can't you keep better control of your men? Or have you trained them to behave like bullies? Sergeant Breen's brutality is matched only by his witlessness."

"Lieutenant, she—" an indignant Breen began.

"Be quiet, soldier!" Stowe barked, interrupting him. "Stand back!"

Breen opened his mouth to protest but Stowe's peremptory gesture and harsh face cowed him. He stepped back as ordered.

"I'll take that gun," Stowe said, holding out his hand to Ki.

"You give it back to Breen," Ki said, "and he might continue trying to fight his undeclared one-man war."

"He won't. I assure you of that. Now, give me the gun."

Ki handed Breen's Colt to Stowe who then handed it to Breen with the unequivocal command, "Holster that sidearm, Sergeant, and leave it holstered until I tell you to do otherwise."

"Yes, sir," Breen responded as he did what he was told.

Lieutenant Stowe bent down to help a still somewhat groggy Howard get to his feet. "I'm truly and terribly sorry for what just happened here, Mr. Howard. Let me assure you that Sergeant Breen shall be properly punished for lack of discipline—"

70

"Not to mention his hotheadedness," Jessie said.

"—and bad judgment," Stowe concluded.

Howard pulled a polka-dotted handkerchief from his pocket and pressed it against his head wound. "I think it's high time you troopers vamoosed."

"We shall leave, Mr. Howard. Just as soon as we have cut twenty head of cattle from your herd."

As Howard started to protest, Jessie said softly, "Joe, I know how you feel. But perhaps it would be better to let him take the stock. You can file a protest with Major Lane at Fort Reno. Better still, you can put your case before Butler at the Darlington Agency. And, if all that fails to remedy the matter, well, I have a few friends in Washington who will be glad to help you collect the money due you for the cattle that have been taken from you to feed the Indians or see to it that such theft is stopped immediately."

Jessie, noting the angry look Stowe gave her when she used the word "theft," said, "That, I submit, Lieutenant, is exactly what it is. Taking cattle from their owners without proper compensation whether done by the army under official orders or by rustlers is nothing other than outright theft."

"Are you accusing me of being a thief, Miss Starbuck?" Stowe practically shouted.

"Yes, I am."

Ki couldn't help smiling as he watched Stowe's face redden and his lips work without managing to speak any words. She's pulled his plug, he thought with barely suppressed glee. Now, what's he going to do about it?

Stowe, drawing himself up and looking for all the world like a pouter pigeon, again ordered his men to cut twenty head of cattle from Howard's herd. His glance flicked from Jessie to Ki to Howard to his men who were busily carrying out his command. Then back again to Howard, to Ki, and finally to Jessie.

"Miss Starbuck," he said, "I could have you brought up on charges."

"What charges and before what tribunal, Lieutenant?" she asked him.

"The charge: interfering with a duly constituted representative of the federal government. The tribunal: a civilian court in Kansas."

"Should you choose to do that, Lieutenant," Jessie said sweetly, "I will press charges against you and your men on behalf of Mr. Howard who has been the victim of harassment and an unprovoked attack by one of your troopers whom you were apparently unable to control. Wouldn't that look good on your military record?"

Mexican standoff, thought an amused Ki.

Stowe took a step toward Jessie who stood her ground before him. Then, his lips pressed tightly together, he turned on his heels and, stony-faced, climbed into his saddle. He ordered his men to move out with the cattle.

They did. So did he.

Howard swore under his breath. Then he apologized to Jessie for having done so.

She patted his arm. "Your words were most appropriate under the circumstances, Joe."

"Well, I reckon it's time I was heading back to my own range, Jessie. If I don't, those troopers are liable to decide to come back and take the rest of my steers. The whole kit and caboodle."

"It's been good seeing you again, Joe. I just wish it could have been under pleasanter circumstances."

"You plan to be on the reservation awhile?"

"Until such time as I can find out what happened to Bob Statler and the others."

"Then maybe we'll meet again. Good luck to you."

Later, as Jessie and Ki unlatched a wooden gate in a barbed wire fence and then relatched it after they had passed through, she announced, "We're on Starbuck range now." She pointed to the star within a circle that had been burned into the gate.

She had no sooner spoken the words when a gunshot shattered the stillness.

The sound sent a roadrunner scurrying out from beneath a juniper bush. It went racing away as a flurry of sparrows went soaring skyward from a shin oak tree.

"That shot came from up around the bend just ahead of us," Jessie noted.

"We'd better not ride on until we find out who did that shooting and why," Ki suggested.

"I agree. There's brush growing up there on the ridge. We can go up there and look down. That way we can see what's around the bend without actually having to travel that way."

"Let's go."

They rode up the slope until they neared the crest of the ridge. There they dismounted and, leaving their horses ground-hitched, crept up to the crest where they flattened themselves on the ground. Peering down, they had a good view of the land below in all directions.

"What's going on?" Ki asked as he surveyed the scene below. "Who's that man and why is he killing those Circle Star cattle?"

Jessie's answer was drowned out by the loud sound of another shot fired by the man below the ridge.

As another cow went down, Jessie repeated what she had just said. "That's Jeff Marsden. He's in charge of Starbuck Enterprises' interests here on our leased land. I don't have any idea why he's shooting those cattle, but I am certainly going to find out. Come on, Ki."

He followed her back to where they had left their horses. Then the pair rode down the slope and around the bend.

"Jeff!" Jessie yelled as they galloped toward the one ranch hand.

He turned, his revolver in hand, and pulled his hat down low on his head to keep the sun out of his eyes as he squinted suspiciously at them.

As his revolver rose, Jessie's hand dropped to her gun butt.

"Jessie!" Marsden's eyes opened wide in surprise as he lowered his gun. "Is it really you?"

As she and Ki drew rein, her hand fell away from her gun.

"It's really me, Jeff."

"I didn't get word you were coming, Jessie, but I sure am happy to see you," Marsden said.

"I didn't send word that I was coming. Now, may I ask why you are killing these steers?"

Marsden looked down at the six cows scattered around the area. Two were on their knees, trying to rise. Two more, which had not been shot, lay dying on the ground, their bodies heaving as they fought for breath. Two others had been shot to death.

"I left the rest of the boys behind," Marsden said, "and came out here hunting this bunch. They wandered away from the main herd. This is what I found when I got here."

Jessie flinched as one of the cows that was lying on its side lifted its head and then let it fall back to the ground. She shuddered as red foam flew from its nostrils. She could barely stand the sight of the agony in the glazed eyes of the stricken animal or the sight of its tongue lolling helplessly out of its gaping jaws.

With a loud flutter of wings, a flock of magpies appeared, seemingly out of nowhere, to alight upon the bodies of both the dead and dying cattle.

A steer bawled weakly as some of the birds pecked mercilessly at its eyes with their cruel black beaks.

Marsden fired again.

74

The tormented steer's skull bloomed like a bloody flower. The magpies flew screeching up into the air, a black and white blur against the bright blue sky. They alighted in a nearby loblolly pine where they began a raucous chattering among themselves, shifting positions, tilting their heads back and forth, twitching their long tails.

"Poison," Marsden said and added, "arsenic." He pointed to traces of white powder that could be seen in the trampled mud surrounding a water hole where the cattle had come to drink.

"Who did it?" Ki asked.

"Don't know," Marsden replied and then shot another steer. "I've no particular fondness for longhorns, but I can tell you this. It rips me up inside to see critters suffer like these have been doing."

He fired again.

A steer's body lurched as if it were about to rise. Then it fell back and moved no more.

Minutes later, Marsden had killed all the steers.

"Indians did it maybe," he said. "They've been stealing stock from us. Now maybe they've taken to poisoning it too. I wouldn't put it past them. That Brave Buffalo and those who think the same way he does, they want all us white folk off the reservation. I'd say it's a good guess that this is the handiwork of the Cheyenne Dog Soldiers. Let me tell you about that bunch, Jessie."

"I know a little about them anyway." Jessie shook her head, a gesture that blended sorrow, disgust, and anger.

"Speaking of Indians," Marsden said, "I've been meaning to get in touch with you, Jessie, which is why I'm glad you're here."

"What about?"

"Things haven't been going too well around here of late. This is not the first time some of our cattle have been poisoned. It probably won't be the last, though I've got all

75

hands on the alert for such goings-on. We've also lost cattle to thieves."

"Indians again?" Ki inquired.

"Can't say for sure and certain," Marsden replied. "Probably. We've lost twenty-three head in the past month. On top of that, we've lost close to fifty to the army. They come and take beeves. They even put us under the gun to do it if we object as I, for one, always do. They tell us the government will pay for the stock they take, but I've not gotten any money for a single head of what the army took off of us."

"We just witnessed an example of what the army can do," Jessie said. "They just took twenty head belonging to Joe Howard. It was a rather ugly encounter."

Marsden nodded. "The only cattleman they don't seem to bother is Chet Lancaster. He's one lucky man, I must say. Anyway, to get to the point, between the thieving and the army taking what they want to feed the Indians over at the agency, we're on the verge of losing money, though our net profit is still pretty good. But this nasty stuff that's been going on"—Marsden pointed to the corpses of the cattle—"it's starting to cut into that profit. If it keeps up at the same rate for much longer, we might find ourselves operating in the red instead of the black."

Jessie felt a hot flush of anger course through her as she thought of Lieutenant David Stowe and his high-handed way with Joe Howard. So he was taking some of her stock too, was he? Her anger grew. Well, she'd see about that and see about it very soon. Tomorrow, in fact. She would also see about the poisoning and theft of her cattle. She did not intend to accept the unsettling losses Marsden had just described to her as merely a cost of doing business. As her range manager had just said, that cost would soon if left unchecked erase, not merely eat into, the grazing operation's net profit.

"We've tried our best to catch whoever's stealing our

stock and sprinkling arsenic out where our cows can get at it," Marsden said. "We've just not had any luck on that score. Except for one time when we came upon two men acting kid of suspicious. We went after them, but it was getting dark. We lost them. Next day two cows died like these here did. We didn't spot the arsenic in the dark, and by the time we got out to the spot early the next morning to have ourselves a look-see, the two critters were as dead as dust."

"I know you're doing the best you can to stop this," Jessie said, glancing down at the dead animals. "I'm going to take a hand in trying to stop it too. First thing tomorrow morning, I'm going to the Darlington Agency and have myself a talk with Amos Butler, the Indian agent, about what's been going on. Much of this may very well be under his jurisdiction. The army's requisitioning of beef and the government's non-payment of the obligations they have thereby taken on is certainly, at least in part, his responsibility. The thieving and the poisoning may turn out to be. I intend to find out, one way or the other."

"But that's not what brought you up here," Marsden commented. "I didn't get word to you about all this, though I was fixing to if things kept getting worse as they do seem to be doing. So why have you come, Jessie?"

She told Marsden about the disappearance of Bob Statler and the herd he had been in charge of. She concluded her account of the matter with a question.

"Did you notice anything amiss when Bob was still here?"

"Not a thing. Bob was his usual jolly self. He was joking like he always does. He even went and put a grass snake in my boot one night when I was sleeping and yelled, 'Rattler!' I tell you it gave me such a scare, I like to have died on the spot."

Marsden smiled sheepishly.

"He was anxious to get to Dodge, he told me," the

range manager continued. "I gather he has himself a lady friend up there. Not a working woman, if you'll excuse the expression, Jessie, but a lady who lives on a farm outside of town. He was fixing to marry her when he got to town this time. He showed me a ring he bought for her over in Darlington just before he left here."

"I didn't know that," Jessie said. "He planned to get married?"

"Sure did. The boys, when I told them on the sly, they harassed him over the matter something fierce, which made me happy as a cow in clover, I can tell you. It was my chance to get even with Bob over that business with the grass snake that made me look the proper fool, running around the way I did in my union suit that night while trying to get away from what I truly did believe was a sidewinder about to take a bite out of me."

"Thank you very much for the information, Jeff," Jessie said. "It puts the matter of the drive to Dodge in an entirely new light for me."

"Do you think something's happened to Bob and his boys?"

"I hope nothing has. But I'm worried."

"Is there something you want me to do?"

"Not at the moment. But, if there is in the future, I'll let you know. Meanwhile, Ki and I will head for Darlington. If you want to get in touch, we'll be staying at the Murray Hotel there."

That night, when Jessie and Ki rode into Darlington, they found the town quiet with very few lights visible anywhere. One did burn beyond the open door of the livery barn and they made their way there.

After arranging to have their saddle horses fed and rubbed down and their pack horse relieved of its burden and also cared for by the sleepy stable boy on duty, they left the livery and made their way to the Murray Hotel.

They climbed the three steps to the hotel's broad porch and went inside. A coal oil lamp burned on the desk next to the door. Behind the desk, in a wooden chair, the desk clerk sat, his hands folded across his ample girth, his eyes closed, his fat lips fluttering wetly as he snored noisily.

Ki, yawning, went to the desk and tapped the bell that sat on it. He had to tap it a second and then a third time before he succeeded in awakening the desk clerk who looked up at him, blinked, and said, "Help you?"

"Two rooms. One for the lady and one for me."

"Two rooms," the clerk repeated and got to his feet. "You're up late, aren't you?"

When neither Ki nor Jessie answered him, he reached behind him and took two keys from separate cubbyholes in a wall rack and handed them to Ki who gave one to Jessie as he yawned again.

The desk clerk slapped a heavy hand down on the bell.

"We don't need any help," Ki told him. "We don't have any luggage."

"Lily, you lazy good-for-nothing," the clerk cried, "get up to room number four and put clean linen on the bed."

Ki stared with interest at the young woman who had just emerged from behind a curtain next to the wall rack at the rear of the desk in apparent response to the clerk's summons. She was pretty in a raffish sort of way, he thought. If she weren't so sleepy, she'd probably have a saucy look about her. She walked in a devil-take-the-hindmost manner that was to Ki both provocative and debonair. She had a don't-give-a-damn attitude that he found appealing. He almost blushed when he became aware that Jessie was watching him closely.

"The linen change won't take long," the clerk declared, settling himself once more in his chair. "Lily should have done it earlier today. I told her to do it. But telling Lily to do something has about as much chance of getting it done as does telling the wind to stop blowing."

"I'll go get clean sheets," Lily announced and proceeded to flounce her way out from behind the desk and across the lobby to a closet on the opposite side of the room.

"Time to turn in," Ki said to Jessie.

"Take my key and give me yours."

"What? Why?"

"Never mind. Just do it."

Ki took the key Jessie was holding out to him and handed her his. Then he stood staring after her, puzzled by what she had just done, as she crossed the lobby and began to climb the stairs to the second floor.

When she reached the landing, she turned and smiled down at him. "Have a good night," she said before turning a corner and disappearing.

Lily slammed the closet door. With clean linen tucked under her arm, she began to mount the stairs, her hand on the railing, moving slowly, sleepily.

Ki, as the desk clerk let out a rumbling snore, crossed the lobby and began to climb the stairs as, above him, Lily turned the corner and vanished from sight. Once on the second floor landing, he looked down at the brass key in his hand. Then he started down the hall, glancing at the numbers on the doors he passed.

Ahead of him, Lily was inserting a pass key in the lock on one of the doors.

Ki passed room number one. Number two. Across the hall was number three. He stopped in front of number four, which matched the number crudely etched on the key in his hand just as Lily opened its door and ambled into the room in which he was to spend the night.

Jessie, he thought, you're a clever one, you are. He recalled the desk clerk ordering Lily to change the linen on the bed in room number four. He recalled the look Jessie had given him as he was watching Lily. Jessie's room had been number four. She had switched keys with him after learning that Lily was to change the bed linen in the room bearing that number. He smiled. Had Jessie done him a favor? He suspected she had as he watched Lily light a lamp, put the clean sheets and pillow slip on a table, and then bend over to strip the dirty linen from the unmade bed, her round rump thrust up into the air and vigorously wriggling.

She looked over her shoulder at Ki who was standing in the doorway and watching her intently. "This won't take long, sir. I'll be finished in just a few minutes and then you can jump into bed and make yourself comfortable."

Did she wink?

Ki decided that it must have been a trick of the flickering lamplight. "Take your time," he told her as he went over and sat down on the single chair in the room. He crossed his legs to hide his hotly throbbing erection.

"Shall I put the blanket on the bed, sir?"

"The blanket?" Lily was staring at him. He crossed his legs in the other direction, right over left this time.

"The nights tend to be cool around here right through till June, sir."

"No, I won't be needing the blanket, thank you."

"You'll be warm enough without it?"

"Hot."

"Beg pardon, sir?"

"It's nothing. Never mind. You're not going, are you?"

"Why, yes, sir, I am. Unless there's something else you want."

"There is." Ki rose and went to Lily who, the bed made, had crossed to the open door and was standing there gazing at him. He no longer cared if she could see the stiff evidence of his arousal. He had to keep her from leaving. But how? He was tempted to seize her, throw her down on the bed, and jump on her. It would never work. She'd probably start screaming. The law or somebody would be sure to come. He'd wind up in jail when all he wanted to do was wind up in her.

"Sir?"

"Water," Ki croaked, consumed now by desire for this very pretty young woman who was looking at him as if she were about to bolt.

"Water, sir?"

"For the pitcher." He pointed to the pitcher sitting on top of the bureau beside a basin.

Lily went and peered into it. Turning back to Ki, she announced, "It's full."

"Oh." What next? What now? Close the window? It was already closed. Scrub the floor? Don't be ridiculous. He surprised himself by blurting out, "You're lovely, you know."

Lily cocked her head to one side. She put her hands on her hips.

Here it comes, Ki thought. She's going to call the desk clerk and accuse me of committing some unspeakable perversion.

"Do you really think so?" Lily asked, the lamplight highlighting her auburn hair and making sparks flare in her brown eyes.

"I was dead beat when I arrived here at the hotel. But seeing you has given me a whole new lease on life."

"What are you?"

"What am I?"

"I know you're not an Indian, but your skin's not exactly as white as snow. You can't be a Negro. You're far too fair-complected for that. Besides which, your hair's as straight as a poker. I know. You're Chinese."

"Close but not correct. My mother was Japanese. My father was an American. I've got both Oriental and Caucasian blood in my veins."

"It looks to me like you wound up with the best from both sides of your family. I mean you're as pretty as a just-painted wagon." Lily took a tentative step in Ki's direction. "I'll bet you'd be about as much fun, once a girl got to know you, as two pups in a basket." She took a bold step in his direction.

He went to her and put his arms around her waist. He drew her close to him. "I'd like to get to know you. I'll bet *you'd* prove to be as much fun as *four* pups in a basket."

Lily, without turning around, kicked the door shut.

After that, things moved quickly. She helped Ki undress, even bending over and facing away from him so he could put one foot after the other on her rump while she pulled his boots off. Then she proceeded to undress and to pull on his still-throbbing erection.

He led her to the bed, and they lay down upon it side by side. She never once released her hold on him.

"Let go," he whispered to her. "I'm so close to coming that if you keep holding on to me so tight it's going to be all over before it has a chance to truly get started."

"We wouldn't want that to happen, would we?" Lily cooed coyly and kissed Ki on the lips, taking his tongue and sucking on it when he thrust it past the easily breached barrier of her teeth.

He fondled her body, her full breasts, her lush hips, her slightly rounded belly, her lean arms and legs. When their kiss ended, he lowered his head and put out his tongue to touch her nipples, which immediately hardened as a result of his attentions.

He cupped her mound with his right hand as he began to suck on her breasts, first one, then the other. She was more than moist; she was wet. He shifted position and eased into her, his passage made smooth by her juices, which bore mute but eloquent testimony to her own arousal.

"Oohhh," she moaned as he sank in her. And, *"Oohhh,"* again she moaned as he began to ride her.

Her moans soon gave way to a series of lusty grunts as she wrapped her arms and then her legs around him. Her fingernails clawed at his back. Her calves encircled his

83

thighs. Her rhythm expertly matched his. Its tempo steadily increased.

The bed beneath them shook. Their bodies slapped sweatily against one another.

Ki felt a gathering in his loins. His shaft became the center of his world, the source of intense and nearly incredible pleasure.

He felt Lily's body spasm beneath him in a prolonged convulsion as she came. He continued his thrusting, his skin beginning to tingle and twitch as she caressed his back and buttocks with her smooth hands.

Her pelvis slammed up to meet him, and she held it there, taking the force of his passion, her body trembling, her head thrown back, her eyes closed, an expression of utter ecstasy on her face as she climaxed a second time.

Ki came a moment after she did. Then he continued bucking for a full minute as Lily settled back on the bed.

"You're better than I had hoped for," she murmured in his ear. "It must be the blending of the blood that makes you so . . . so exciting."

He held her close to him, his body on fire, his thoughts burning. Those thoughts kept him stiff inside her.

"You're a long way from finished, aren't you?" she whispered in his ear.

"A long way," he agreed, hoping.

Lily came through for him. "This time I'll get on top if that's all right. Is it?"

It turned out, a delighted Ki discovered, to be far more than merely all right. It turned out to be fantastic.

★
Chapter 6

At dawn the next morning, but before the sun had risen, Jessie left her room, locked her door, and started down the hall of the Murray Hotel.

When she reached room number four, she raised her hand to knock on its door. Before she could do so, the door opened, and Lily backed out into the hall.

Because she was paying attention to where she had been and not to where she was going, she collided with Jessie.

"Oh!" she cried. "I beg your pardon, Miss. I was just . . . I wasn't—"

"Is he awake?" an amused Jessie inquired.

Lilly shook her head. "He was up most of the night."

Realizing what she had said and how it could be interpreted in more than one way, she clapped a hand over her mouth.

Jessie couldn't help herself. She laughed.

"You're not mad at me, Miss?"

"No. Why should I be mad at you?"

"For—you know—being with Ki last night. I know you and he—"

"No, Lily, I'm not mad. You're making an incorrect assumption about Ki and me. He and I are friends, very good friends, and have been for years."

"Just friends?"

"Nothing more."

"Oh. I thought—"

"You say he's sleeping."

"Yes, Miss. He's tuckered."

"I wonder if you would do me a favor, Lily."

"I'd be glad to."

"When Ki gets up and comes downstairs—you'll be there?" When Lily nodded, Jessie continued, "Tell him I've gone to the Darlington Agency to meet with Agent Butler. Tell him he's welcome to meet me there if he wishes to do so."

"I'll be sure to tell him, Miss. I'll be on the lookout for him. He won't get past me."

"I don't imagine he would want to, Lily. You're a very attractive young woman."

"Oh, it's nice of you to say so. Do you mind, Miss, if I say something personal to you?"

Jessie waited.

"You told me there wasn't anything between you and Ki—"

"Except friendship."

"Yes. Well, I think you're lucky to have such a friend. I've known a lot of men in my time, sad to say. With most of them, after they've had their way with you, it's goodbye and nice to have known you. But Ki, he's not that kind of man. He treated me real fine. He treated me like I was a lady and not just some baggage he ran into and rolled around with for a spell."

"Ki is a very kind and compassionate man, Lily."

"Yes, he is all of that and then some."

"Now, do you mind if I say something personal to you, Lily?"

"No, I don't mind, I don't think."

"Why did you call yourself baggage just now?"

"Because, I suppose, that's what men have called me, some of them."

"So you have taken on the identity those men have given you. Do you think that makes sense? You're an attractive woman and a nice person. Ki treated you the way you deserve to be treated. Why don't you try thinking of yourself the way he thought of you last night? It might work wonders for you."

Lily smiled the smile of a child who has just been told she's not only loved but also admired.

The sun was hot when Jessie rode across the last mile of the flat plain that seemed to stretch endlessly around her and arrived at the Darlington Indian Agency that was bordered on one side by the North Fork of the Canadian River.

There was a solid row of buildings in the distance, and she headed straight for them, passing as she rode on an occasional tepee or isolated wooden building. Just this side of the western horizon, she saw an Indian encampment. The place looked deserted.

When she reached the cluster of buildings, she drew rein in front of one of the wooden buildings, which, she knew, housed the agency. Like the others, the building was unpainted and beginning to rot in places. She dismounted and left her horse with its reins trailing so that it would stand and not run off.

She knocked on the door of the building and a mild voice called out, "Come in."

She went inside, and once her eyes had adjusted to the dim light inside the building, she was able to make out the thin, almost gaunt, figure who was standing beside an open doorway and peering at her through a pair of spectacles that kept sliding down his beak of a nose, forcing him to push them back into place again, a necessary little ritual that he performed constantly and without variation.

"I'd like to speak to Agent Butler," she told the man who stood, she estimated, only a little over five feet tall.

He pushed his spectacles into place and meekly declared, "I am Amos Butler. How may I help you?"

She wanted to answer, "You can keep the Indians in

your charge from stealing cattle that belong to me," but she didn't. There would be time for that later. After she had attended to the matter that was uppermost in her mind.

"Mr. Butler, my name is Jessica Starbuck."

Before she could say anything more, Butler said, "Miss Starbuck, I have heard a great deal about you and Starbuck Enterprises over the years. You have quite an enviable reputation in the nation. In fact, I knew of you years ago when I was working at the Department of the Interior in Washington. I knew your illustrious father then, and he always spoke most fondly of you. I was most distressed to learn of his untimely passing.

"I should tell you that I received a telegraph message recently regarding one of your drovers and his men and the herd they were taking to Dodge City."

"I want to thank you for your prompt reply to that inquiry, Mr. Butler. A subsequent message from the cattle broker we do business with in Dodge informed us that Mr. Statler—"

"Your drover."

"Yes. We were informed that he never arrived in Dodge nor did the herd that was in his charge. I've come here to investigate what can only be called, I think, the disappearance of the herd and the men responsible for it. I came here this morning to ask you if you had any other word concerning the matter since the message you sent in response to our original inquiry."

"I'm so sorry, Miss Starbuck. I'm afraid I must disappoint you. I have had no additional word of any kind from any source. As I mentioned in the message I sent, your Circle Star herd arrived here and your men left with fattened cattle for Dodge some time ago now. I venture to say they should have reached Dodge quite some time ago if nothing untoward has happened to prevent them from doing so."

Jessie's disappointment at what Butler had to tell her

must have shown in her face, because the agent hastened to add, "I can also tell you nothing about the person you specifically inquired about. What was his name? Billy McLean?"

"MacKenzie."

"Yes, that was it. Billy MacKenzie. I'm afraid I did not then and do not now know anything about him or, in fact, about any of Mr. Statler's men or Mr. Statler himself. You see, I have very little to do with the cattlemen who use parts of the reservation's land for grazing purposes other than in a purely administrative and fiduciary capacity. Your Mr. Statler did meet briefly with me to make the semiannual payment due for the use of your leased land, as I believe I stated in my telegraph message."

"I've made inquiries, specifically of Mr. Chet Lancaster and Mr. Joe Howard," Jessie said. "I've learned from Mr. Howard that he saw the Circle Star herd heading north. I suppose the thing I must do at this juncture is take the trail to Dodge myself and see if I can locate them somewhere along the way."

"That might be a wise thing to do. I truly hope that there is nothing seriously wrong. It may well be that they have been merely delayed in their journey. Such may indeed be the case, you know."

"There are other matters, three, actually," Jessie said, "that I wanted to bring to your attention, Mr. Butler."

"Oh? Do they have something to do with the Indians here on the reservation?" Butler shoved his wayward spectacles back up on his nose and blinked at Jessie through them. "If they do not, I'm afraid I can't help you in any official way. Though I shall be glad to listen sympathetically to whatever you have to say."

"I've been given to understand from my range manager that we have lost a number of head of cattle to thieves lately. We have also had some of our cattle poisoned by arsenic. I myself came upon some dying steers only yesterday on my way to Darlington. It has been suggested to me that Cheyenne or Arapaho Indians or both might have been responsible."

The mouse of a man that Butler appeared to be suddenly turned into a lion, albeit a small one of not very striking stature. "Do you have proof of these allegations, Miss Starbuck?" His tone was sharp; his eyes were cold.

"No, but—"

"I am tired of hearing unwarranted, not to mention unproven, accusations being made against this reservation's Indians. They are not villains, I assure you, Miss Starbuck, although I shall be the first to admit that they have been at times, ah, difficult.

"When you consider their plight, a people uprooted from their homelands and brought here, a people whose way of life has been disappearing because of the incursion of white people onto their lands and into their lives—"

"I understand what you call the plight of your charges, Mr. Butler. I ask only that you try to understand my position as a businesswoman."

"I do understand your position. No one wants to suffer losses. But you admit you have no proof that your cattle have been stolen or poisoned by Indians. You jump much too readily to conclusions, I fear, Miss Starbuck."

"I have jumped to no conclusions, Mr. Butler. I have come here today simply to ask you to look into the matter. You are the one person best qualified to get to the bottom of this problem. You know the Indians. You work with them on a daily basis. You are obviously concerned about them and their well-being. I assume they will talk to you if you make inquiries concerning the points I've just raised."

Butler sat down in a chair next to his desk. "Have a seat, Miss Starbuck. Forgive me for my outburst. I am a weary man," he continued as Jessie sat down. "Weary of fighting the bureaucracy in Washington and at the Central Superintendency in Lawrence. Weary, too, of being forced to make do with too little food for the Indians, too little medicine for their ills, too little compassion and understanding for the psychic pain that is a very real part of their everyday lives. I suppose I should be strong. I thought I *was* strong when I first came here. Now I know I am not. Now I know that I have not only bent under the pressure of trying to make do with too little that always seems to arrive too late to help the Indians, but I know also that I am about to break under the strain."

"I understand that yours is a difficult position."

"Difficult? Nay, Miss Starbuck, it is an impossible position."

"I'm sorry to hear of the problems you're having in administering the agency." What am I talking about, Jessie asked herself. I came here to get my problems solved, not to listen to Amos Butler's problems.

But she couldn't help feeling sorry for the man. His, she knew, was a virtually thankless task and one that would have tried the patience, and ultimately broken the spirit, of a saint.

Butler surprised her by looking her directly in the eye and remarking, "It was probably my Indians who stole your cattle."

"But you don't know that for sure, I take it."

"No, I don't know it for sure. But the Indians are hungry. Miss Starbuck, what would you do if your life had evolved and revolved around the buffalo for an uncounted amount of time and then white men came to your country and began to systematically and quite successfully slaughter the beasts until, for all intents and purposes, there are no more buffalo?

"Once, I am told, they darkened the plains. Once it took hours, they say, for a herd to pass a given point. Now they are gone, almost all of them, and they will not be back. Soon we may find ourselves saying the same thing about the Cheyenne and the Arapaho and all the other Indians

God put on this earth apparently to suffer under the onslaught of a relentlessly advancing tide of white settlers.

"Miss Starbuck, the Indians used the buffalo not only for food but also for clothing, shelter, weapons, tools, utensils, religious and recreational equipment. What are these people to do now that the very basis of their lives and culture, the buffalo, is gone and we bureaucrats can do little or nothing for them despite our very best intentions?

"Don't bother to answer my question. It was a rhetorical one. On the other hand, it was not at all rhetorical but quite definitely a pragmatic question. I think the answer to it is a sad and sorry one. What must a people do when the very foundation of their civilization disappears? They must die, Miss Starbuck. They must die a slow and ignominious death of both the body and the spirit."

"That brings to mind the third matter I wanted to discuss with you, Mr. Butler," Jessie said, noticing that the agent seemed lost in a sad-eyed reverie, so lost, in fact, that he had not bothered to push up his spectacles, which had slipped down to a precarious point at the very tip of his nose.

"Mr. Butler, did you hear what I said?"

He looked up at Jessie. "What?"

"I wanted to discuss a third matter with you. It has to do with the requisitioning of beef from the various herds grazing on reservation land. I understand that you issue orders concerning the taking of beef from the herds of various stock owners such as myself. I have learned that the government has failed to pay for the stock they have taken, forcibly in some cases, from us. I was wondering what comments you might care to make concerning this situation."

"I do have a comment or two to make concerning it," Butler said, returning his errant spectacles to their proper place on his nose. "The Cheyenne and Arapaho are hungry. No, it's worse than that. They are starving. I've already explained to you that there are virtually no buffalo for them to hunt anymore. I authorized a hunt recently and they found but two buffalo. That is hardly enough to feed the many Indians living here on the reservation."

"I'm sorry to hear that the Indians are suffering," Jessie said sincerely. "And I, for one, am not protesting the turning over to the government—to the Darlington Indian Agency—beeves that are needed to feed a starving people. What I am protesting on my behalf and on behalf of other cattle owners is the failure of the government to pay promptly, or, in many cases, to pay at all for those cattle."

"I do not handle the agency's accounting, Miss Starbuck. That work is done by my most able assistant, Mr. Mark Demming. I shall summon him; he has an office here in the building. He will be able to tell you what he knows about any payments that may be due for the beef we have obtained from the herds grazing on Indian lands. If you'll excuse me for a moment . . ."

Butler rose and left the room. He returned moments later accompanied by a man Jessie judged to be in his late twenties. He had a mustache that was as bushy and red as his hair and he was smiling in a way that made her feel uncomfortable. His smile did not soften the glassy glint in his pale blue eyes.

"Miss Starbuck," said Butler, "may I present Mr. Mark Demming. Mark, Miss Jessica Starbuck who, as you know, is one of our lessees."

"A pleasure, Miss Starbuck," said Demming in a silken voice that Jessie nevertheless found irritating. He took the hand she offered him, but instead of shaking it, he bent and kissed it. He held it a moment, looking into her eyes, and then he stepped back and said, "Mr. Butler tells me you're interested in our beef acquisition program."

"That's a rather innocuous name for what some might call a confiscation program, Mr. Demming," Jessie responded somewhat irritably, annoyed by Demming's smoothness, which bordered on oiliness.

"What's in a name, as the poet says, eh, Miss Starbuck?" quipped Demming. "What is it you wanted to know about the program. Specifically, I mean."

"What I wanted to know specifically, Mr. Demming, is why you—Mr. Butler has told me you are in charge of the matter—have not seen to it that the cattle you have arranged for the Fourth Cavalry to take from us are not paid for in a timely fashion."

"I can offer in my defense only the fact that the matter is largely out of my hands. I do promptly submit vouchers to the Bureau of Indian Affairs at the Department of the Interior in Washington, but I'm afraid they are most notoriously slow in rendering payment.

"I have written numerous letters and sent many telegraph messages requesting payment but, alas, to little or no avail, as you have just so correctly pointed out."

"What else can be done to see that the owners of the cattle receive the monies due them—and receive them promptly, Mr. Demming?" Jessie prodded.

"Nothing, I'm afraid."

"Nothing? Really, Mr. Demming? I would think that, in the interests of maintaining good relations with your lessees, you might want to take funds from your agency's operating expense budget to pay the cattle owners and then replace that money with the funds you later receive from Washington."

"That strikes me as a capital idea, Mark," Butler declared.

Demming placed a finger against his nose and stared thoughtfully at Jessie for a moment before stating, "It could be done, I suppose. But at some cost."

"What cost, Mr. Demming?"

"Yes, Mark, explain yourself, if you please," Butler said.

"Well, as you know, Amos, we are never flush with funds, to speak in the argot of the gaming table," Demming drawled, tapping his finger against his nose. "We might well find ourselves perilously short of basic operating expenses were we to pay the cattle owners out of our budget and then have to wait until Washington sends the funds to pay for the previously acquired cattle."

"Mark makes a pertinent point," Butler told Jessie. "We scrimp and scrape to get by on a month-to-month basis as things stand now. Our budget for the entire operation of this agency is not by any means what could be called munificent."

"I would take this opportunity, gentlemen, to point out to you that some cattle owners are beginning to suffer financially as a result of the things I've been discussing with you here today."

In a quick aside to Demming, Butler explained, "Miss Starbuck has mentioned the matters of the Indians stealing and poisoning cattle."

"Brave Buffalo and his Dog Soldiers, no doubt," Demming snapped.

"Hold on," Jessie said. "Let me make one thing clear. I never accused anyone of poisoning or stealing stock for the simple reason that I do not know who has been doing it. I merely brought the matters up in the hope that you gentlemen would look into them and, if possible, put a prompt stop to them. As I said before, some of us leasing land here are sufferering financially as a result of these problems, these problems combined with the additional one of the government taking our cattle at will without ever compensating us for them. It is a situation that cannot go on without having serious fiscal implications for more than one herd owner."

"Look into all this, will you, Mark?" Butler requested. "At your earliest convenience?" He proceeded to tick off on his fingers the three matters of concern to Jessie: "The poisoning of lessees' stock; the theft of stock; the failure to render prompt payment for stock."

"I'll do so at once, Amos. You may depend upon me."

"I want to express my appreciation to both of you gentlemen for your kind cooperation," Jessie said, rising. "I know you will want to get in touch with me concerning your findings. I'm staying, for the time being, at the Murray Hotel in Darlington."

Demming made a graceful grab for her hand and kissed it a second time. Butler bowed her out of the office.

As she descended the steps from the porch, Butler, standing behind her in the open doorway, said, "You have come here at an auspicious time. You will be able to witness the good use to which the cattle we acquire are put on beef issue day. Gooday, Miss Starbuck."

Jessie stood on the bottom step and watched as scores of Indians came running from every direction toward a huge corral in the distance. She watched the detachment of Fourth Cavalry troopers, under the command of Lieutenant David Stowe, slowly drive a herd of cattle toward the corral where the Indians, armed with bows and guns and knives, were waiting.

She estimated the herd contained forty head, give or take a few. Approximately twice the twenty steers Stowe and his men had cut from Joe Howard's herd.

She walked slowly over to the corral as the Indians surrounded her, shouting, calling out to one another, dancing gaily together on the dusty ground, and, she noticed, buying whiskey from a peddler who was selling it openly from the back of a wagon, well within sight of the agency's offices. The man was performing this illegal act with glib disregard for the authorities who were nowhere in sight.

Indians arrived in wagons and on foot, more and more of them. Most rode in on horses. One Indian family arrived in a surrey.

The crowd grew rapidly. It was composed of men,

women, and children, and even a few infants in cradle-boards. Jessie was soon hemmed in by it and almost caught up by the holiday atmosphere surrounding beef issue day.

Once inside the corral, with the gate closed behind them, the cattle milled, their great eyes rolling in fear, which was being caused by the din around them. They thudded against one another and against the poles of the pen. They bawled loudly, their horns clattering against those of the animals next to them.

Jessie looked up and met the impassive gaze of Brave Buffalo who stood opposite her on the far side of the corral. His arms were folded across his brawny bare chest, his black braids were hanging down his back. He looked away —at nothing that Jessie could see. He seemed to be present and yet not present, as if he were above the melee surrounding the corral. He also seemed to be displaying an open contempt for the proceedings.

"One animal to a family!" Lieutenant Stowe called out. "Watch your line of fire. We don't want any accidental injuries. Get ready!"

A momentary hush fell on the crowd. Men raised rifles and pistols and bows.

"Get set!"

The air suddenly filled with the harshly metallic sound of shells being levered into the chambers of rifles and the hammers of six-guns being cocked.

"Fire!"

The sound of gunfire deafened Jessie as the Indians fired at the prey that was penned helplessly inside the corral. A few beasts fell following the first volley. Others staggered about, wounded. Still others, unhurt, wheeled frantically in a desperate but futile effort to escape their fate. One steer tried but failed to leap to freedom over the poles of the corral.

The firing erupted again amid loud shouts of joy. More steers went down. Blood flew through the air to stain the onlookers who didn't seem to mind as they kept cheering and clapping their hands.

Finally, the last steer fell and lay twitching on the ground.

The slaughter finished, Lieutenant Stowe climbed up on the corral poles so that he towered over the crowd and shouted, "Claim your kills!"

The corral gate was swung open, and amid whoops of jubilation, Indians flooded into the enclosure. Within minutes, several fights had erupted as two or more Indians disputed angrily among themselves regarding the rightful claimant of a dead steer.

Troopers were promptly dispatched by Lieutenant Stowe to break up the fights and arbitrate the disputes, which they did effectively.

The butchering began.

Indians skinned their kills, some of them waving the stripped and bleeding hides in the air like festive banners. Haunches and shoulders were removed and quickly carried away by Indian women along with other parts of the dead animals' bodies. One Indian ripped the lifeless heart from a cow and greedily devoured it on the spot, triumphantly thumping his chest with his fists as he did so.

"You have come to see the beggars."

Jessie, startled, turned to find Brave Buffalo standing next to her.

"I beg your pardon?"

Brave Buffalo, with a sweep of his arm that encompassed the Indians inside the corral who were busily butchering the dead cattle, said, "Beggars. Not hunters. These men who have forgotten how to be men come and take what the white man chooses to give them."

"You have not claimed your kill?"

"I make no kill. I do not want the bone that white Indian agent throws to his red dogs."

Jessie found herself both impressed with the obvious

98

pride that Brave Buffalo possessed and simultaneously disturbed by the bleak future that fierce pride of his would inevitably place before him.

"If you do not take some of this beef, you and your family will go hungry," she argued.

"I have no family. No woman. No children."

"What about yourself? How do you live?"

"I hunt. Me and my Dog Soldiers, we hunt together."

"What do you hunt?" Jessie asked as an Indian inside the corral whooped and swung a portion of a steer's carcass onto his shoulder, spraying her jacket with droplets of blood in the process.

"We hunt rabbits. Skunks. We fish. We survive."

"Agent Butler told me about the problems your people are having since the buffalo have been nearly all killed by white hunters. What he did not tell me was that there were men like you who manage to survive in the old ways."

"Men like me," Brave Buffalo repeated as he stared intently at Jessie. "Yes, there are still left some men like me who will not beg from the white man. Who will not approve of turning our land over to your people so that you can use it to make money. But there are also men who are not like me. They are like the half-bloods and the Indians who have intermarried with the whites. They see a new moon in the sky. I and my warriors, the Dog Soldiers, we see the old moon still, the one that was in the sky when we were first put here on this land. We do not see the new moon of the others who call themselves men but whose blood has turned from red to white."

"I admire the way you stand up for what you believe in. What I don't admire is that episode on the plain yesterday when your stole four of Chet Lancaster's steers."

"We did not steal them."

"I *saw* you steal them."

"You saw us take them in trade for the four ponies the white man, Jim Hanson, stole from Has Horses. It was a

fair thing to do. When we could not have Hanson to pun-
ish, we take steers instead. Share with other Dog Soldiers
and their families."

"You had no proof that Jim Hanson stole Has Horses's
ponies," Jessie argued.

"Not so. We have proof. Has Horses see Hanson steal
ponies. His woman see Hanson. His daughter also see it
happen."

"But what you should have done is taken Hanson to
court, as Lancaster suggested. Let Has Horses and the
members of his family who witnessed the crime testify to
what they saw. You can't just take the law into your own
hands."

"You speak of white men's law. Agent Butler say he has
no money to pay for Has Horses and his family to go to
Kansas where the white man's law is. So we do what must
be done. We settle things Indian way."

Jessie could think of no more to say. Too often she had
seen justice sold to the highest bidder. What Brave Buffalo
had done was clean and neat. She had to admit that to
herself. A fair trade, as he had suggested, even though it in
now way fit or met the niceties of the white man's law with
its courts and judges and juries. In fact, the way Brave
Buffalo had finally chosen to settle the matter of the crime
he claimed Hanson had committed was, she thought, probably better than if he and the others had taken personal
vengeance on Hanson, the alleged thief.

"You would do well, I think, to accept at least some of
the ways of the white people," she advised the Cheyenne.
"I know it is hard, and I know too that your ways—the old
ways—have much merit. But consider this. Things are
changing and changing fast. If you and your people do not
change with them, they—you—will suffer. I don't want
to see that happen to any of your people or to you."

When Brave Buffalo—who stood so proudly, almost
regally, she thought, before her—said nothing, she added,

"I wish my men were herding buffalo instead of cattle. I would gladly tell them to let some of their stock go so that you and your people could hunt them. But you must see that what I have just said is, at best, foolish and, at worst, harmful. It would be little different than what has happened here today, something you would not accept."

"You are like the soldiers, the settlers on our land, the herders who let their cattle eat our grass, the Indian agents who come here and tell us to do this and not to do that. Sit here. Stand over there. You say you want to give us what is good for us. But what you give us costs too much. It costs a man his dignity, and it teaches him a terrible lesson—how to live his life on his knees."

As Brave Buffalo turned sharply and strode away from her, Jessie tried to think of something to say to him but the words, at least none that she considered to be the right ones, came to her mind.

She felt embarrassed as a result of their encounter. She felt humiliated by what she recognized as the inescapable truth of the man's eloquent words. She felt ashamed that she too was a part of a system that exacted such an awful price from the Indians who wanted nothing more than to be left alone in the land they believed was theirs.

She turned to watch the butchering that was continuing to take place inside the corral. Some of her stock, she now knew, had once been butchered in this same corral and would be again if the agency and the army had its way.

Brave Buffalo was right. She was like the others who were, in one way or another, destroying not only the Cheyenne and Arapaho Nations but also a way of life she suspected was, in some important ways, better than the ones most white people lived.

★
Chapter 7

"Is he a friend of yours?" Lieutenant Stowe asked as he joined Jessie and nodded in the direction of the retreating Brave Buffalo.

"No. We were just talking. Why do you ask?"

"Well, he's not exactly friendly to people like us, him and the men who ride with him."

"You mean, I take it, white people."

"That's what I mean all right. Brave Buffalo and his Dog Soldiers, they do have a way of causing headaches and heartaches for people around here if their skin happens to be white."

"What do you mean exactly?"

"Brave Buffalo and some of his Dog Soldiers stole four steers from Mr. Chet Lancaster yesterday and then stampeded the rest of his herd."

"How do you know that?"

"I was talking to Lancaster."

"He told you that Brave Buffalo and his men stole his steers?"

"He did."

"He told you that the Indians stampeded his herd?"

"He did."

"And you believed him?"

"Why wouldn't I believe him?"

"I suppose I shouldn't have asked that question. Of

course you'd believe him. You'd have no reason not to do so."

"Miss Starbuck, just what are you getting at?"

"The Dog Soldiers didn't steal Lancaster's steers. They took them in payment for the ponies they claimed Jim Hanson, one of Lancaster's hands, stole from a Dog Soldier named Has Horses. As for the stampede, Lancaster's own men caused it by shooting wildly at Brave Buffalo and the other Indians with him in an attempt to stop what they considered to be a theft of their property."

"You say 'what they considered to be a theft.' Are you perhaps implying that you don't consider the act a theft?"

"As a matter of fact, I don't. Has Horses claimed to have witnessed the theft of his ponies as did, he said, his wife and daughter. Brave Buffalo wanted to take Hanson to court in Kansas but Agent Butler had no money, as it turned out, to pay for them to make the trip there. So the Indians took the matter into their own hands.

"At first, they asked that Hanson be turned over to them. When Lancaster refused that demand, they took the four head of cattle as recompense for the ponies they insist Hanson stole from Has Horses."

"A highly irregular procedure, wouldn't you say?"

"I suppose it is irregular, as you put it. But what else could the Indians do? They wanted justice. They got it, as far as I'm concerned. Lancaster won't miss the four steers they took and the Indians' sense of justice and personal honor have been satisfied. What's most important, no one was hurt during the confrontation."

"Unlike other instances of similar encounters between cattlemen and Cheyenne Dog Soldiers," Stowe said.

"What other instances are you talking about?"

"Oh, there have been several run-ins of one degree of severity or another of late here on the reservation between Brave Buffalo and white men. There was, to give one example of what I'm talking about, the time they caught a white trader raping one of their women. They fixed him in a hurry—and in more ways than one."

"What do you mean?"

Stowe blushed. "I'd rather not say."

"They scalped him? Killed him?"

Looking away from Jessie, Stowe said softly, "They fixed him so he wouldn't rape another of their women or any other woman—ever."

"I see."

"Then there was the shoot-out with some drovers that took place over a week ago at Bennett's Pass on the Western Trail."

"What drovers are you talking about?" Jessie quickly asked.

"I was out on patrol with my men that day. You know, don't you, that the Fourth Cavalry is charged with keeping the peace here on the reservation?"

"Tell me what happened."

"We came upon the drovers and Brave Buffalo and some of his Dog Soldiers. Both sides were at loggerheads. It seems that the Dog Soldiers wanted the drovers to leave the Western Trail and to travel to Dodge by one detour or another because, according to the Indians, the drovers were on grassland that belonged exclusively to the Dog Soldiers.

"Now, the drovers, on the other hand, didn't want to lose valuable time. On top of that, they insisted that they had a perfect right to travel the Western Trail to Dodge and that no 'heathen Indians'—that's what Statler called the Dog Soldiers—were going to stop them from doing just that."

Jessie seized Stowe's arm. "You said, 'Statler'."

"Yes, I did. Why do you ask? What's wrong?"

"A man who works for me is named Bob Statler. Is he the one to whom you just referred?"

104

"Yes. He introduced himself to me after we sent the Indians packing."

"When you left Statler, was he all right?"

"He was fine."

"His men? His herd?"

"Everything was fine. A shot or two had been fired on both sides but no one was hit. There were more hot words thrown around that day than there was hot lead."

"But there was bad blood between Statler and the Indians?"

"Yes, there was. Where, may I ask, is all this leading?"

"Bob Statler, together with his men and their herd, have disappeared. They never got to Dodge City. Joe Howard told me he had seen them heading north. Now you tell me Statler had a run-in with the Cheyenne Dog Soldiers."

"You think the Indians ambushed them farther up the trail?"

"I don't know what to think, to be honest about it."

"Those Indians are hotheaded fellows. They may have backed off just long enough to see me and my troopers ride away. Maybe then they went after Statler again."

"You said before that this incident took place at Bennett's Pass on the Western Trail, didn't you?"

"That's right."

Jessie started walking back the way she had come, heading for the building that housed the Indian Agency.

Stowe followed her, hurrying to keep up with her. "What are you going to do? Nothing rash, I hope."

"Lieutenant, I came all the way up here from Texas to find out what happened to Statler and his men. You have just given me information that is worth looking into. I'm going to ride out and have a look around the Bennett's Pass area and due north of that spot to see what, if anything, I can find out. Then I intend to go and talk to Brave Buffalo. I want to confront him with the information you have just given me. Right now, I am going to leave a message with Agent Butler for my friend, Ki, who may be coming to meet me here. I also want to find out from Mr. Butler where I can locate Brave Buffalo."

"I can tell you where to find him," Stowe volunteered.

"Where?"

"He lives in a small village about three miles northwest of here with other Dog Soldiers and their families. They're a clannish lot. They stick together. Can't blame them for that, I suppose, since most of the other Cheyenne Indians here have abandoned the old ways and consider their warrior societies—the Dog Soldiers very much included—passé."

"Thank you for the information, Lieutenant."

"Miss Starbuck, it's none of my business but I would urge you not to go to the Dog Soldiers' village alone. There's no telling what might happen to you if you do."

"I appreciate your concern, Lieutenant. But I'm perfectly capable of taking care of myself."

"Well, you know what they say."

"What do they say, Lieutenant?"

"A word to the wise is sufficient."

"Goodbye, Lieutenant. It was nice seeing you again."

"Miss Starbuck, I want you to know that I would gladly go with you but I am duty-bound to return posthaste to Fort Reno with my troopers to report to Major Lane."

"I understand."

As Lieutenant Stowe turned to leave, Jessie went inside the agency building where she left a message for Ki with Agent Butler.

When Ki arrived at the Darlington Agency later that day, he asked the first person he met, an aged Indian seated in the shade of a building, where the agency was located.

The Indian pointed wordlessly to the building he was seeking, and Ki rode up to it, dismounted, and went inside.

"My name is Ki," he told Agent Butler who was seated

at a desk and taking official-looking documents from a drawer. "I'm looking for Miss Starbuck. Can you tell me if she's here?"

"I'm afraid not."

"Does that mean you can't tell me if she's here or does it mean she's not here?"

"Oh, dear, I really should be more precise in my speech. I am Amos Butler, the Indian agent." Butler held out a hand to Ki who shook it. "Miss Starbuck was here but she has gone. However, she did leave a message for you in case you came here looking for her, sir. I have it here somewhere." Butler began to root through piles of papers in search of the message. "I know it's here. I put it here myself. So many papers. So much red tape." He *tsk-tsked*. "Ah, here it is." He handed a slip of paper to Ki.

Ki took it, unfolded it and read:

"Ki:
    Urgent business required that I leave before you arrived. Will meet you later back at the hotel.

                                 Jessie"

"You're a friend of Miss Starbuck?" Butler asked.

"Yes, I am."

"Remarkable woman. Remarkable. I was quite impressed with her. We had ourselves quite a little chat while she was here."

"Did she say where she was going?"

"No, she didn't."

"Thank you, Mr. Butler."

"Good day to you, sir."

Outside, Ki hesitated a moment and then, not wanting to have made the trip for nothing, decided to ride north and have a look around the area where the cattleman, Joe Howard, had last seen Bob Statler and his men as they were journeying north.

Maybe, he thought, by scouting the area, I might be able to find something that will give me an idea of what might have happened to Statler and the others. It might turn out to be a wild goose chase. The trail was cold. But it was worth a try. Nothing ventured, nothing gained, he told himself as he swung into the saddle and rode north.

As Jessie rode along the bank of a twisting stream, she realized that the relentless spring sun, hot today as on any day in mid-summer, was making her thirsty. She drew rein and slid out of the saddle. Her horse needed no urging. It followed her over to the water's edge and, as she knelt down and caught some water in her cupped hands, the animal lowered its head to drink also. Horse and rider drank deeply after which Jessie got back in the saddle.

She rode on, passing some low hills on her right, and then rode in among a stand of shin oaks, which offered her brief relief from the hot hammer of the sun in their deep shade. She was reluctant to leave the grove but leave it she did. As she emerged from the trees, she saw tepees in the distance.

The Dog Soldiers' camp, she thought. As she angled northwest, the camp was on her right, and the sun was in her eyes. She pulled her hat down low on her forehead to shield her eyes from the glare and rode on.

Fifteen minutes later, she had reached the draw that wound its circuitous way between hills on either side of it—hills that were little more than high hummocks.

She rode through the draw that went by the name of Bennett's Pass and then out of it. She halted her horse and looked around. At the ground. At the vegetation growing in the area—scrub pine and juniper mostly. She saw nothing notable. She turned her horse and rode back through the pass, and then when she emerged from it, she began to ride in an ever-widening circle, searching for she knew not what but scanning the ground for a sign. She kept a sharp lookout for the ashes of old campfires and for anything that might in its mute way speak to her of what had happened to Statler and his men.

Half an hour later, fighting off a sense of futility that bordered on despair, she headed back the way she had come. Her hunt was a frustrating one because it had been fruitless.

The sun was high in the western sky as she passed a herd of Indian ponies peacefully grazing a half mile east of the Dog Soldiers' camp under the watchful eyes of a young Indian boy of no more than fourteen or fifteen.

Later, as she rode into the camp of the Dog Soldiers, she pretended to ignore the stares of the Indians who watched her pass by, some of them clearly hostile. She was saddened by the sight of the bulging bellies of many of the children, the visible mark of undernourishment and hunger. Those bellies bulging beneath buckskin garments, combined with the blank stares of the dull-eyed people watching her ride by, both shamed and angered her.

You're not responsible for them, she told herself. But the admonition did not help ease her sense of sorrow.

A young woman with lustrous black hair, unbraided, came out of a tepee and stopped short when she saw Jessie, her eyes widening with what might have been alarm.

"I'm looking for the lodge of Brave Buffalo," she told the young woman. "Do you know where it is?"

The woman turned and quickly reentered the tepee.

Jessie was about to ride on when a resonant male voice spoke from behind her.

"What do you want here?"

Jessie glanced over her shoulder and saw Brave Buffalo standing some distance away. "You," she answered.

"Go away."

Jessie slid out of the saddle and, leading her horse, walked up to Brave Buffalo. "I will go when you have answered some questions for me."

109

Brave Buffalo merely stared at her for a moment, the mask of his bronzed face unreadable, before turning and striding away.

Jessie, still leading her horse, hurried after him. When she caught up with him, she stepped in front of him to block his path.

"Did you and your men ambush my drovers?"

Brave Buffalo pushed past her. She caught up with him again and repeated her question.

"Who are your drovers?"

Jessie described Brave Buffalo's encounter with Statler and his men as it had been related to her by Lieutenant Stowe.

"We ambush no drovers," Brave Buffalo said curtly when she had finished her account.

"Are you telling me the truth?"

Something flashed in Brave Buffalo's black eyes.

He's furious with me, Jessie thought, but her gaze did not waver. She had to know what, if anything, this man knew about the fate of her employees.

"You ask if I speak truth. I tell you this. Cheyenne children sometimes lie. It is the way of children. Both Cheyenne men and women of honor do not lie. Tell truth."

"You did have a shoot-out with my men," Jessie accused.

"They shot at Dog Soldiers."

"Lieutenant Stowe said shots were fired on both sides."

"Has Horses was with us that day. He dropped his gun. It fired."

"Tell me your version of what happened that day."

"You come here. Give orders. I do not take orders."

Jessie warned herself to back off. It was obvious to her that she was dealing with a very proud man, and it was equally obvious to her that she had just offended that man's pride. But she wanted to hear what Brave Buffalo would say about the encounter with Statler and the cavalry to see if his version matched Lieutenant Stowe's account of what had happened.

"I'm sorry," she apologized. "It is just that I am worried about those men who were with the herd that day. One of them is a fifteen-year-old boy, and all of them seem to have vanished. I came here to try to find out what has happened to them. To do that I will need all the help I can get. That's why I came here to ask you about the incident we have been discussing. You might be able to tell me something that would throw some light on the matter of my missing men."

"You believe what I say before?"

"About you and your men not ambushing the drovers?" Jessie hesitated. Did she believe Brave Buffalo? Had he told her the truth? Was he the honest and honorable man he claimed to be? "I believe you," she said finally and saw his features relax into something that was almost a smile.

"I will tell you what happened though it shames me. We try to make your drovers leave reservation land. They would not leave. Has Horses drew his gun. He dropped it. It went off. Your men, two of them, they shoot at us. We ready to shoot back when cavalry comes and says we must go away. They have many guns. We have only two. Mine and Has Horsess'. We give in. We go."

Jessie noted the bleak look that had come into Brave Buffalo's eyes as he spoke his last words.

"One more time the white man turns Indians into tame dogs who creep away after they have been beaten."

Jessie had begun to feel increasingly uncomfortable as she listened to the Cheyenne. She was finding it difficult to face the man and his obvious shame because she hated to see a brave and virile man like Brave Buffalo humiliated.

"Thank you for telling me this," she said. "I must go now."

For a moment, she thought Brave Buffalo was going to say something to keep her from leaving. She waited a split second, and then when he remained silent, she swung into the saddle and rode out of the camp, resisting the urge to look back over her shoulder at the man she found herself irresistibly attracted to.

She was approaching the spot where the Indians' pony herd was grazing when she thought she saw something moving in among the loblolly pines behind the boy who was guarding the ponies.

Just shadows shifting as the trees sway in the breeze, she told herself. And yet . . .

She slowed her horse and peered at the pines. The boy was hunkered down not far from them, his arms folded across his upraised knees. She studied the stand of pines.

Something was moving through them!

A figure suddenly emerged from the trees and crept toward the boy. Another boy? No. Too tall.

Jessie began to feel a sense of impending danger. There was something about the moving figure that seemed familiar to her, but she couldn't see the face of the man who was fast approaching the boy who was guarding the herd.

The man scooped something up from the ground and then went running toward the herd boy.

Jessie was about to shout a warning, but it was too late to do so she realized. The rock the man had scooped up from the ground slammed down on the boy's skull, and he toppled over and fell to the ground.

The man turned, ran back into the pines, and emerged from them a moment later aboard a big bay. It was then, as Jessie recognized the horse, that she knew who it was who had struck the herd boy, although she still could not see his face.

It was Jim Hanson who worked for Chet Lancaster. The man accused of having stolen Has Horsess' ponies.

And that was precisely what Hanson was about to do now, Jessie realized. He was about to steal more ponies from the camp's collective herd.

As she began to gallop in Hanson's direction, she was able to make out the man's features as he quickly cut several head from the herd and began to drive them away.

She drew her Colt as she shortened the distance between herself and Hanson and shouted to him.

"Hold it!"

Hanson looked back and saw her. Saw, too, the gun in her hand. He quickened his horse's pace, lashing the animal with his reins, driving the Indian ponies before him in a frantic attempt to escape from his pursuer.

When he saw that escape was impossible, he drew his own gun, turned in the saddle, and fired a snap shot at Jessie.

She ducked down, clinging tightly to her horse's neck, and the round went harmlessly over her head.

But Hanson's second shot, following hard upon the first, grazed her mount's left leg, causing it to stumble and almost fall. Jessie held on as the horse swayed under her. When it began to slow, she dug her heels into its flanks and kept it going.

Up ahead of her, Hanson suddenly turned and began galloping back toward her, his gun raised and aimed directly at her.

She took aim at him and fired. But she missed her target—Hanson's gunhand.

"Drop it!" he barked as he rode up to her, his gun aimed at her midsection.

Her finger began to squeeze the trigger of her weapon. She wanted more than anything else at that moment to blow Hanson away for hitting—perhaps seriously injuring or even killing—the Indian herd boy and for having tried to kill her as she tried to stop his escape with the ponies he had stolen.

"Drop it!" Hanson repeated. "Do it, missy, or I'll drop *you!*"

Jessie reluctantly let her gun fall from her hand.

"Move out. No, not that way, the way those horses I was driving went."

Jessie rode in the direction Hanson had indicated. "Where are we going?"

"We're going to put some distance between us and those savages back there. I don't want them interfering with what I got in mind."

As Hanson leered at her, Jessie decided she knew what he had in mind. "My horse is hurt," she said. "He can't travel far." It was partially a lie, and she wondered if Hanson knew it was.

"We don't have much farther to go. Once we get there—you know something? I had it hard for you from the very first minute we met."

When Jessie didn't respond, Hanson continued, "It's hard as iron right now, missy, and I can tell you I'm going to have a whole lot of fun with you before it gets soft again."

They rode on until they reached the horses that Hanson had stolen. The animals stood near a low limestone ridge, grazing and moving about almost listlessly.

"We'll stop here," Hanson announced. "Get down out of that saddle."

Jessie dismounted with alacrity, and before Hanson was out of the saddle, she slapped his mount's rump.

The animal bolted.

"Hey!" Hanson yelled as he was thrown to the ground.

Before he could speak another word, Jessie sprang upon him and began trying to wrest the gun from his hand.

"You *bitch!*" he screamed as he slammed a hand into her face, his palm and widespread fingers pressing against her flesh and forcing her head backward.

He screamed then as Jessie bit his hand. As he quickly withdrew it, she kneed him in the groin. He let out a shrill yell and clutched his genitals with his free left hand. She continued struggling to gain control of the gun in his right hand, and she almost had it when he suddenly jerked his hand free of her grasp and struck her with the barrel of his gun.

Pain blasted through her neck where the weapon had landed and raced up into her skull and down into her chest. She gasped for breath, her eyes beginning to water.

Hanson shoved and scrambled out from under her. As he was getting to his feet, Jessie tackled him. He fell, rolled over and, holding his gun in both hands now, fired at her.

More pain invaded her body, beginning at the site of the flesh wound in her upper left arm where Hanson's round had entered and exited.

She sprang to her feet and kicked out. Her right foot smashed into Hanson's gunhand, sending his weapon flying through the air.

She and Hanson both grabbed for it. Jessie got it. Hanson twisted her wrist violently in an attempt to retrieve the weapon. As he did so, the gun's barrel swung toward him and his hand, which was pressing Jessie's, caused her finger to tighten involuntarily on the trigger.

The blast was muffled since the barrel of the gun was pressing against Hanson's chest.

He looked at Jessie in surprise. He opened his mouth to speak but blood, not words, slid from between his lips. A moment later, the blood stopped flowing, indicating to Jessie that his heart had stopped pumping. His eyes grew glassy. He fell back on the ground, his arms lying lifeless at his sides.

Jessie, feeling faint from the pain that was burning within her, got shakily to her feet and looked down at Hanson. Then she examined the wound in her arm. It was still bleeding but no bones had been broken. She drew a deep breath and thrust Hanson's gun under her belt. Then she proceeded to lift Hanson's corpse and throw it over his horse's saddle. When she had done so, she stood there, leaning against her wounded horse and trying to ignore the pain in her arm and neck. Sweat beaded on her forehead. For a moment, the world went dark but then it abruptly brightened again. She took another deep breath and then stepped into the saddle.

Hazing the Indian ponies before her and leading Hanson's horse, she backtrailed until she reached the spot where she had dropped her gun. She slid out of the saddle, holstered the gun, and resumed her journey.

When she reached the spot where Hanson had attacked the defenseless Indian herd boy, she found that the youngster had vanished. She looked around but saw no sign of him. Wondering about the boy's whereabouts, she headed for the Dog Soldiers' camp.

Long before she reached it, she saw Brave Buffalo riding out of the camp and heading straight for her.

When they met, he looked first at her wounded arm and the blood that had crusted on her torn buckskin jacket, then at Hanson's corpse, and then directly at her, an unspoken question in his eyes.

She answered it. "I caught Hanson trying to steal some of your ponies. He struck your herd boy with a rock. The boy was gone when I looked for him."

"Boy is with his mother. He is not hurt bad. You wait here."

Brave Buffalo proceeded to drive the horses Jessie had retrieved from Hanson to where the rest of the herd was still quietly grazing. Then he rode back to Jessie, beckoned to her, and said, "You come."

"I can't. I have to return to Darlington. I—"

"You come."

Jessie was about to protest again but then thought better of it. She would see what this man had in mind.

As it turned out, Brave Buffalo had her wound in mind. Once in the camp, he gave orders to a squaw and a boy. The boy went running toward the horse herd, and the squaw, with a firm gesture, indicated to Jessie that she was to step down from her saddle.

She did, and then followed the beckoning squaw into a nearby tepee. Half an hour later, her wound had been cleansed and bandaged by the Cheyenne woman.

"Thank you," Jessie told the woman who was gathering up her cloths and bowl of hot water. "Thank you very much. My arm hardly hurts at all now."

She doubted that the woman could understand her, but she hoped she could convey her gratitude by smiling at the woman, which she did as the squaw threw back the flap of the tepee and went outside.

"Wait!" Jessie called out to her. She followed the woman outside.

There, the squaw held up a hand, its palm facing Jessie. An unmistakable gesture that clearly meant she was to return to the tepee.

She did so, but her patience was running out. She was about to make another attempt to leave when Brave Buffalo entered the tepee. He stood just inside it, staring at Jessie.

"Thank you for getting that woman to help me," she said.

"Woman say you not hurt bad. Heal quick."

"I hope your herd boy's head will also heal quickly."

"Boy say he wake up after Hanson hit him. See Hanson take ponies and you away. He run here to tell me. Say he heard shooting. I go to get my horses back from Hanson."

"I like that!" Jessie exclaimed, her patience giving way to anger. "You were more worried about your horses than you were about me!"

When Brave Buffalo did not speak, she added, "I'm leaving. Now! Get out of my way."

She tried to shove the Cheyenne aside but he was unmovable. Trying to maintain her badly dented dignity, she said, "I asked you to get out of my way."

Brave Buffalo reached out and took her in his arms.

"You will not leave my lodge. Not yet." He bent his head and kissed her. "This is the way white men do with their women, yes?"

Jessie, taken aback by Brave Buffalo's sudden and unexpected action and made breathless by his passionate kiss, could only nod.

He kissed her again.

Jessie embraced him with her uninjured arm, and then as desire exploded within her, she also put her wounded arm around him, unmindful of the momentary pain the action caused her.

Brave Buffalo kissed her cheeks, her throat, her hair. He ran his hands over her body, seeking and finding what he so eagerly sought.

Jessie's hands slid down his back to grip his buttocks and hold him close to her.

Moments later, they dropped down on a buffalo robe and quickly shed their clothes.

Brave Buffalo wasted no time. He gripped his erection and slid it into Jessie who lay back on the buffalo robe with her legs spread wide and welcoming. When he was entirely within her, he whispered, "You were wrong. It was not my horses I was worried about. It was you."

His words sent a thrill of pleasure coursing through Jessie, which was heightened by the way he had begun to swivel his lean hips as he impaled her where she so willingly lay.

"I'm glad," she whispered, and then moaned as she felt herself rising toward a climax.

Brave Buffalo slid his arms beneath her back and pulled her closer to him. His head nestled between her neck and shoulder. His tongue and lips caressed her throat as their bodies blended ryhthmically.

Jessie threw her head back, her coppery hair haloing around her head, as she gave herself over totally to the experience of being possessed by this wild Indian who

118

made her feel ten times a woman and thoroughly thrilled to be one.

They lay then on the buffalo robe together, their bodies still joined, both their chests heaving with the exultant exertion of their lovemaking, Brave Buffalo's strong bronze body pressed against Jessie's lithe white one.

Time passed. The world turned.

Jessie began to move sensuously, her fingers lightly caressing her lover.

Brave Buffalo mumbled something and sighed contentedly. His loins grew warm, then hot. He began again to buck and moments later Jessie cried out as she climaxed.

Brave Buffalo, when his turn to climax came a few minutes later, let out a series of yelps that bore vivid testimony to the degree of his sexual arousal and the ecstasy of the release he was experiencing.

When they both had quieted and were lying side by side some minutes later, Brave Buffalo touched Jessie's lips with one finger, a light caress, and whispered, "Some day, somehow, I will repay you for stopping Hanson from stealing Dog Soldiers' horses."

His words barely registered with Jessie. She was lost in a lush daydream of a dark but benevolent god of brazen delights whose name was Brave Buffalo.

★

Chapter 8

After riding east from Darlington across the land leased from the Indians by Starbuck Enterprises, Ki reached the boundary the Circle Star range shared with Joe Howard. There he turned north onto the Western Trail. Soon he reached the spot where Howard had earlier stated that he had met and rode with Bob Statler and his drovers for a time as they all headed north.

"As I understand it," Ki told his horse, "the place where Howard left Statler and rode north on his own isn't far from here."

The horse nickered softly, it ears erect.

Ki traveled past limestone slopes that were bare of any kind of vegetation and over vast flat tracts of fertile land on which short grasses grew, forming a verdant green landscape that stretched for miles in all directions.

He continued doggedly following the Western Trail, which was the highway for many herds traveling from Texas through Indian Territory to Dodge City. The route favored by drovers, the Western Trail originated in San Antonio, Texas. The Circle Star herds always took this trail if their destination was Dodge.

Ki thought back, recalling the conversation he and Jessie had had with Joe Howard, the cattleman who was their neighbor to the west in the leased lands.

Howard, he recalled, had said that after leaving Statler, he had ridden north and then, upon returning south, had seen no sign of Statler, his men, or the herd. Howard had speculated that Statler must have decided, for some unknown reason, to leave the Western Trail. Otherwise, he would surely have met Statler again on his way back to his own range.

Now why would Statler want to leave a well-worn trail like the Western that he knows as well as he knows his own name, Ki asked himself. To get out of somebody's way? To lie low to keep out of somebody's sight?

Ki remembered that Chet Lancaster had suggested that Statler might have run into Indian trouble during his journey north.

He considered that possibility. It could have happened. But someone, sooner or later, would have found out about it and reported it to the authorities at Darlington. To Agent Butler, for example. If that had happened, Butler certainly would have told us about it, Ki reasoned.

None of this made much sense, he finally decided. Even if Statler, for one reason or another, had chosen to leave the trail, he certainly would not have vanished as if he and his men and their cattle had stepped off the edge of the world. No, it simply wouldn't wash.

If there had been Indian trouble, how was it that no one, apparently, had heard a word or a whisper about it?

Shaking his head in bewilderment, Ki rode on, scanning the ground around him in all directions as he searched for the men and cattle that seemed to have disappeared like smoke in a Texas blue norther.

When he estimated that he had covered the nine miles that Howard had said he had traveled in his hunt for strays, Ki drew rein and sat his saddle, gazing at the vast empty land around him.

A wild goose chase, he thought. I ride all the way up here and nothing. But dammit there has to be *something!* Statler has to be somewhere and so do the cattle he was driving. Howard said he had ridden with Statler for a while, and then because the herd moved slowly, he had ridden ahead in the same direction the herd was heading—north—to hunt for his strays. He found them nine miles from the place where he had left Statler, he had said, and then he had turned around and started back down south along the Western Trail. The trail Statler had been on! Which, in my book, Ki mused, means that Statler had to have disappeared somewhere between here and nine miles south of here.

There's just one thing I can do at this point, he thought. And that's check both sides of this trail for a nine-mile stretch between here and where Statler and Howard first hooked up together.

He turned his horse and rode west. For the next several hours, as the sun rose higher in the sky and then began its slow descent toward the western horizon, he crisscrossed the Western Trail, riding several miles east and west of it. He found the remains of a cow and a calf. He found the skeleton of a dead Indian wrapped in a blanket and placed in a tree in the manner of the Cheyenne. The deceased was a woman, he knew, because her cooking pots, digging stick, and hide-fleshing tool lay on the ground beneath the skeleton.

He found a dead campfire, its ashes still warm.

He found no sign whatsoever of Statler and his men and no sign of the herd they had been driving.

He slowed his horse to a walk and covered the last mile that remained to be searched. Any hope he might have had of finding what he had been looking for had faded away completely by the time he started back toward the trail. He was riding along a ridge that had a steep dropoff on the left when he saw, or thought he saw, a flash of light.

It had flared so briefly that he wasn't sure where it had come from at first. It had barely registered in his consciousness. He turned and looked behind him. Nothing. He looked down. Nothing.

Wait! There was something. Another flash of light that lasted no more than a second or two. It had come, as had the first one, from somewhere within the tangle of trees and thick underbrush below the ridge.

What had caused it? Ki didn't know. But he intended to find out. He knew he might be chasing a will-o'-the-wisp but a will-o'-the-wisp was more than he had found to chase so far today.

He dismounted and, moving cautiously, began to descend into the gorge below the ridge. He slipped and slid his way down, clutching at trees stunted by the winds that ripped through the gorge, trying to keep himself from falling headlong into the chasm below.

When he reached the bottom, he found himself standing nearly thigh-deep in underbrush that hid the ground. He plowed through it once he had gotten his bearings and began to search for whatever it was that had flashed in the light of the sun.

It took him some time but he finally found it. A belt buckle with a steer's horns etched on it.

The belt buckle belonged to Billy MacKenzie whose clothed body lay only partially covered by the underbrush. Time, the elements, animals, and insects had all done their ugly work on the remains. As they had on the other bodies, Bob Statler's among them, that Ki found scattered about in the dense underbrush.

Somebody hid them down here, he thought. If they had fallen from the ridge up above, they'd be lying on top of the brush down here and easy to see from up there. No, somebody hauled them down here and shoved them under the brush. It was pure dumb luck that the sun struck Billy's belt buckle and I happened to be on hand to see it flash. If I hadn't seen it, these bodies would most likely never have been found.

He examined the bodies more closely in the next few minutes. He found spent rounds on the ground and in the remains. He also found two arrows, one of them in Billy MacKenzie's body, one in the body of another drover.

Indians. Either Cheyenne or Arapaho. Maybe both.

He withdrew and began to climb back up to where he had left his horse on the ridge. He had to tell Jessie. He didn't want to tell her. He didn't want to be the bearer of such very bad news. But it was something he had to do and he would do it.

That night, after returning to Darlington, Ki knocked on the door of Jessie's hotel room.

She opened it a moment later and, smiling, said, "Come in."

Ki followed her into the room and closed the door behind him. "I'm sorry I missed you at the agency, Jessie."

She sat down in a chair next to the bed. "I went to Brave Buffalo's camp to find out if his Dog Soldiers—if he—had anything to do with the disappearance of Statler and the others.

"Brave Buffalo denies that he or any of his men had anything to do with it. At this point, Ki, I must say that I believe him.

"It turned out to be quite an exciting afternoon out there. I was leaving when I came upon Jim Hanson trying to steal some of the Indians' ponies that were grazing outside of camp. I went after him, and to make a long story short, we had a bit of a gun battle. Hanson wounded my horse, but it's nothing serious. He'll heal. Hanson is dead. That's his revolver over there on the dresser.

"I turned Hanson's body and horse over to Chet Lancaster before coming back here. When I told him what Hanson had done, he was shocked. He said he would have fired Hanson on the spot had he known the man was a horse thief."

When Ki remained silent, Jessie commented, "Is something the matter?"

124

"Jessie, I found them."

"You found Statler and his men?"

"Yes, I did."

"Where are they? Are they all right?"

"They're in a gorge northwest of here. And no, they're not all right."

"Not all right? Are they . . . are you saying they're . . ."

"Dead," Ki said when Jessie failed to finish her sentence.

"Oh, no! What happened to them?"

"I don't know. I do know they were shot to death. With both bullets and arrows."

"Indians!"

Ki said nothing.

"Brave Buffalo lied to me," Jessie said in an almost inaudible voice. 'He insisted neither he nor his men had had a hand in Statler's disappearance. He played me for a fool, Ki. I believed him. I really did. He seemed so sincere. While all the time . . ."

Jessie got to her feet and began to pace the room. "What about the herd? Did you find it too?"

"No, I didn't. I don't know what happened to it. It may have been taken by whoever murdered Statler and the others."

"Brave Buffalo and his men must have hidden the cattle," Jessie said, her tone bitter.

"We don't know for sure that it was the Dog Soldiers who murdered Statler and the others," Ki pointed out. "It could have been other members of the Cheyenne tribe. It also could have been Arapaho Indians who did it."

"Where exactly is this gorge in which you found them?"

Ki described its location, concluding with, "They were killed somewhere else and dumped in the gorge between the time Howard left them to ride north and his return. Whoever killed them had attempted to hide the bodies. It's an out-of-the-way place. I found them pretty much by accident." He explained to Jessie how he had discovered the corpses.

"Was Billy MacKenzie among them?" Jessie asked, halting her pacing and turning to face Ki.

Judging by the expression on her face, he could tell she was hoping that his answer would be a negative one. She probably hopes, he thought, that Billy quit his job or something before the murders. That he's safe and sound somewhere.

"He was there, Jessie."

Ki watched her bite her lower lip. He saw the tears form in her eyes. Saw them slide slowly down her cheeks before she turned away and went to stand by the window with her back to him.

"That poor boy," she murmured, her voice breaking. "Those poor men."

A moment later, when she turned away from the window to face Ki once more, her tears were gone, and there was a determined expression on her face.

"I want to see the spot for myself," she said.

"That may not be a good idea. It's not a pretty sight. They've been dead for a long time."

"I want to see for myself first thing tomorrow morning," Jessie insisted. "When I have done that, then I intend to go to Brave Buffalo's camp and confront him with what I have seen."

Early the next morning, Jessie and Ki arrived on the ridge above the gorge where the bodies were. Ki offered to help Jessie climb down the steep slope, but she insisted she could make it on her own. Together they made their way down the slope, occasionally slipping when they dislodged loose rocks but managing to maintain their precarious balance.

When they reached the bottom of the incline, Ki led Jessie to where the body of Billy MacKenzie lay.

She stared down at it in silence for a moment and then turned away.

"I told you not to come," Ki reminded her. "It's not a very nice sight." He put his arm around Jessie as she stood there shuddering.

"I'm all right," she whispered a moment later and then turned to look again at the ghastly scene. She remained motionless for some time, and then squaring her shoulders, and taking a deep breath, she bent down and pulled the arrow from the dead boy's remains, dislodging a spent round that fell out of the corpse as she did so.

"What are you gong to do with that?"

As Jessie wiped the arrow clean on the underbrush, she answered, "I'm going to take it to Brave Buffalo and ask him to explain to me what arrows are doing in these two bodies. But first I have to go and see Jeff Marsden."

When they reached the cow camp on the land leased by Starbuck Enterprises, they found Marsden hunkered down by a fire, a cup of coffee in his hands.

He rose and greeted Jessie and Ki as they rode into camp. "You two are early risers, looks like, to get all the way out here with the sun just barely up and awake its own self."

"Jeff, I'm afraid I've got bad news," Jessie said after dismounting and, with Ki, joining Marsden at the fire.

"Bad news?"

"We found Statler and his men," Ki said.

"They're dead," Jessie added.

Marsden, his coffee forgotten, looked stricken. "What happened to them?"

"We don't know," Jessie said. "They were shot. With both bullets and arrows."

"Indians."

"Cheyenne Indians would be my guess," Jessie said, "but I can't prove they did it. Not yet. I can't. I'm on my way to have a talk with Brave Buffalo, the chief of the Cheyenne Dog Soldiers."

"That Brave Buffalo has been agitating to get us and every other cattle outfit off reservation land ever since I got here. Him and his boys, they've been known to steal beeves too. They say they need them on account of they'd starve without them. They've taken some of ours as I think I told you. I'm just itching to catch them at it. If—when I do there'll be a few dead Indians to bury, I can guarantee you that."

"Speaking of burying," Jessie said, "that brings me to the reason for my visit. Jeff, I'd appreciate it if you'd round up some of your men and see to it that Statler and the others get a decent burial."

"Sure thing, Jessie. I'll take care of that right away. Where are the bodies?"

Ki told him where they were located.

"Jessie," Marsden said angrily, "are you fixing to see to it that Brave Buffalo and his boys get what's coming to them for what they did?"

"When I'm sure they're the guilty ones, yes."

"That's good news. It's high time somebody cut that Brave Buffalo down to size, him and the other marauders who ride with him."

Jessie was deep in thought as she and Ki rode toward the Cheyenne camp. She felt she had been used by Brave Buffalo. Worse than that, she felt debased by him. She had given herself freely to him, and he had betrayed her. She now believed that he had known all the time they were making love in his lodge that Statler and the others were lying dead in the gorge, their bodies pierced not only by bullets but also by Indian arrows.

Anger directed at the man coursed through her, inflaming her cheeks and shaping her lips into a grim line. She kept her eyes on the tepees in the distance, afraid to glance in Ki's direction because, knowing her as well as he did, she was sure he would probably guess correctly what she was feeling as well as the reason for that feeling.

As they passed the grazing ground which the Indian horse herd used, the tepees loomed larger against the horizon. When they rode into the camp, Jessie led the way to Brave Buffalo's lodge where she dismounted as did Ki.

She called out the Dog Soldiers' chief's name and then waited until he emerged from his lodge a moment later.

She ignored the smile that brightened his face when he saw her. She also ignored the friendly greeting he gave her, and she ignored too the uneasy look that replaced his smile when she did not respond to his greeting. Forcing herself to speak slowly and without heat, she said, "I have something to show you." She held up the arrow.

Brave Buffalo looked at it and then at her again.

"You told me you knew nothing about the disappearance of my men," she stated bluntly.

"That is so."

"Ki found them. They're dead, all of them, including a fifteen-year-old boy. This arrow was in the body of that boy. There was another arrow in the body of another drover. Now, do you still maintain that you know nothing about those men and what happened to them?"

Brave Buffalo's face darkened as if the sun had suddenly disappeared from the sky. His eyes seemed to grow blacker. More penetrating.

"I told you the truth," he said, his gaze on Jessie, his arms folded across his chest.

"*This* is the truth!" she exclaimed, holding the arrow up and shaking it in his face.

"You think I shot that arrow into the boy you spoke of?"

"You made no secret of the fact that you want white cattle owners off reservation land," Jessie pointed out. "You had a run-in with my men."

"That is true."

129

"You have stolen cattle—"

"That is not true. Dog Soldiers have never stolen cattle. We did not steal your herd. I told you. We hunt. We do not steal meat from white intruders. Others maybe steal. Not Dog Soldiers. Not me."

Jessie felt her resolve weakening. As she stared at the man in front of her, she recalled the ecstasy they had shared only the day before. She wanted desperately to believe what he was saying, but she had lost confidence in Brave Buffalo and was no longer able to believe what he told her.

Laughter suddenly burst from his lips. It was soft but decidedly derisive.

Anger returned to Jessie as he stood there laughing at her.

Before she could give voice to the fury that was surging within her, Brave Buffalo stopped laughing and said, "You white people know nothing but you act as if you know everything. You see arrow in dead body and so you say Cheyenne killed this man. You say I have proof. See, I have arrow in my hand that I took from dead body. You are foolish."

Jessie was struck dumb not only by the words Brave Buffalo had just spoken but also by the contemptuous way he had spoken them.

"What is it we do not know, Brave Buffalo?" Ki asked. "Is it something about the arrow?"

Brave Buffalo studied him for a moment before remarking, "Woman speaks words of fire. You speak words like cool water."

"You know something," Ki said. "What is it? Don't tease us. Tell us what you know."

Jessie started to say something but Ki silenced her by holding up a hand while never taking his eyes from Brave Buffalo's face.

"This arrow not made by Indian," the Cheyenne declared. "Bad work. No Indian make such a bad arrow. This is not Cheyenne arrow. See the shaft. It is tipped with feathers of crow. If you were wise in the ways of the Cheyenne, you would know crow is sacred bird of Cheyenne. We would never use feathers of crow on our arrows. It would be like white man spitting on Christian cross. Do you know why other Indian tribes like Shoshoni and Comanche call us 'the striped arrows people'?"

"No," Ki admitted. "What are you getting at?"

"They call us the striped arrows people because Cheyenne warriors use turkey feathers on the shafts of our arrows."

Jessie said, "I didn't know—"

"No, you did not," a grim Brave Buffalo interrupted. "Maybe so you should have known so that you would not come here and say Cheyenne killed your men when they did not.

"If we killed your men, we would have done as we always do to those we kill. We would cut off one finger, maybe so more than one. Maybe so one hand. Maybe so both hands."

Brave Buffalo drew his right index finger several times across his left forefinger.

"What are you doing?" Jessie asked him.

"That is Cheyenne tribal sign. It means 'cut fingers' or 'cut wrists.' It is the sign that tells of what Cheyenne do to those we kill."

"I owe you an apology," Jessie told the Cheyenne. "I'm sorry for losing my temper and jumping to what was obviously the wrong conclusion about who was responsible for the deaths of my drovers. I really am very sorry."

"Wait a minute," Ki said. "Maybe this eliminates the Cheyenne as the killers of Statler and the others but it doesn't eliminate the Arapaho."

Brave Buffalo snorted. "You know nothing about what you speak. Crow is also sacred bird of Arapaho. They

131

would not dare to use sacred bird's feathers on arrow shafts just as Cheyenne people would never do so."

It was Ki's turn to apologize to Brave Buffalo, and he did.

"You must look in another place if you are to find who killed your men and stole your herd," Brave Buffalo said, addressing Jessie.

"To tell you the truth," she said sadly, "I have no idea how to find the murderer or murderers."

"I know how," Brave Buffalo declared confidently.

"You do?" Jessie stared at him, a question in her eyes.

"Find the cattle that have been stolen. They will tell you who killed your men."

"That's a thing that's a lot easier said than done," Jessie remarked. "Those cattle could be anywhere. They could even be in a holding pen at a Kansas railhead or on their way to a slaughterhouse there."

"Maybe," Ki mused. "Maybe not."

"What do you mean?"

"People who buy cattle in Dodge know the Circle Star brand. If whoever stole them were to try to sell those cattle without a legitimate bill of sale, it wouldn't work. The buyers would suspect that the stock had been stolen. They wouldn't touch them with a ten-foot pole."

"It might be worth trying to find out if they're still being held here on the reservation somewhere," Jessie suggested. "Of course, it's a task that's pretty much like trying to find a needle in a haystack. But I'm willing to give it a try. What about you, Ki?"

"I'm willing to have a look around. Not so much for the sake of finding the herd—that's a loss that can be either written off or made up in future stock sales—but for the sake of finding out who killed the drovers so they can be made to pay for what they did."

"My sentiments exactly," Jessie declared. "We can

cover more ground more quickly if we split up. Does that suit you, Ki?"

"Sure. Suppose I check out the area north of here and you take the southern range, Jessie."

"We'll meet back at the hotel tonight. If neither of us finds anything, we can try again tomorrow."

Ki stepped into the saddle and rode away.

"I will go with you," Brave Buffalo said to Jessie.

"I thought you wouldn't want anything more to do with me after the things I said to you."

"Words in the wind. Blown away now. All forgotten."

A few minutes later, Jessie and Brave Buffalo left the camp of the Dog Soldiers and rode south.

★

Chapter 9

Ki rode for hours during which time he examined every herd of cattle he came upon for any sign of the stolen Circle Star stock. He found none, although his sharp eyes did detect the presence of several head of cattle in a herd belonging to a man he met by the name of Ralph Farley that bore a brand different from Farley's own brand, a Lazy F. He said nothing to Farley of what he had noticed, and the two men parted amiably.

He considered it better to say nothing about the fact that Farley and his hands were, apparently, not above a little rustling on the side. Which, he knew, was by no means an uncommon practice. A man riding his range would find a few head of cattle that had strayed onto his property. He would simply appropriate them and alter their brands. Or he would discover some yearlings on his land that had not yet been branded. He would see to it that they bore his brand in very short order.

When Ki heard the sound of cattle lowing off to his right, he rode in that direction. He topped a rise and saw them down below him. He made his way down the slope and slowly circled the herd, noting brands as he went. Nothing out of the ordinary. The stock all bore the same brand: a Flying T.

When he spotted one of the herd's outriders heading toward him, he changed direction and headed back up the slope and down the other side of the rise. He had no time to waste on small talk. Nor did he want to arouse any suspicions among the lessees who were using reservation land for grazing.

By late in the afternoon he had checked, by his count, a total of eleven herds. With the single exception of the cattle that were mixed in with Farley's and bore a brand other than Farley's own, he found absolutely nothing at all out of the ordinary.

He looked up at the sky and, judging by the position of the sun, estimated that it was nearing five o'clock. He decided it was time to return to Darlington. The sun would soon be down, and he could not accomplish his purpose in the dark.

One last stop, he told himself as he headed southeast. I'll be riding across Joe Howard's range. Might as well have a look at his herd on my way back to the hotel. I never did see any of his stock that day we met when he was out rounding up strays.

He found Howard's cow camp less than an hour later. It was located on the boundary that separated Howard's range from Jessie's. There were only two men in it besides Howard himself, which Ki found strange. But then he decided that the other men must either be out with the cattle somewhere or else driving them north to Kansas.

He halloed the camp before riding in, and Howard returned his greeting. Only then did he ride in, and even then he did not dismount.

"Light and cool your saddle," Howard said.

"Thanks, I think I will. I've been riding a long time, and I'm just this side of saddle sore."

"What are you doing in this neck of the woods?"

"I'm looking for the Circle Star stock that Jessie told you she had lost."

"You haven't found them yet?"

"Not one of them." And I guess, Ki thought, I'm not going to find them among your holdings since none of your stock's in sight. "We did find the drovers though." He told Howard about the grisly discovery he had made in the gorge.

Howard listened without expression as he spoke, but when Ki had finished his account, he swore volubly. "We all need our heads examined," he muttered. "A man has to be loco to stick it out here. The grass isn't worth the game."

"I'm not sure I follow you, Mr. Howard."

"I'm talking about losing stock to the Indians either through them stealing them themselves or the government stealing them from us and handing them over to the redskins. A man can't make a decent profit over the long term with such shenanigans going on. That's why I've quit playing the god damned game."

"You're leaving?"

"You just bet I am. I'll be glad to shake the dust of this place off my feet, I can tell you. I've sublet my range to Lancaster and sold him what cattle I had left at a loss. Most of my men have gone to work for other cattlemen. Me, I'm going back home to Texas. From now on, I'm driving cattle straight through the Nations and on into Kansas. They'll be a lot skinnier when they get there but at least nobody will be stealing them from me."

"I'll tell Jessie you're leaving."

"You do that. You can tell her something else, if you've a mind to."

"What's that?"

"Tell her I think that Indian agent, Amos Butler, is behind all this. I think he's playing it real cute with the government and with Lancaster."

"I don't understand."

"I told you and Jessie that Lancaster's herds never get bothered by the army when they're on the prowl looking for beef. If you ask me, Butler's the one who gets the payments due on the cattle that the government, with the able and willing help of the cavalry, takes from us. I've never gotten a damned dime in return for all the beef that the army has taken from me. Tell Jessie she'd better keep a sharp eye out so she doesn't get taken like the rest of us— all save Lancaster—have been."

"Do you have any proof that Mr. Butler is dishonest or that he deliberately leaves the Lancaster herd alone when he needs beef for his Indians?"

"No, I don't. Oh, I know what you're thinking. You're thinking that what you just heard from me is a sour grapes story. Well, I'm here to tell you it's not. Something funny's going on around here, and I think Butler has a hand—*both* hands—in it along with Lancaster."

"I'll be sure to tell Jessie what you had to say about Butler and Lancaster, Mr. Howard. I wish you luck in the future."

"My luck's bound to get better," Howard muttered. "It sure as hell can't get any worse than it's been."

Ki climbed aboard his horse and rode west at a gallop, heading for Lancaster's range. He had originally planned to check the Lancaster herd in the morning, as he had checked other herds today to see if it included any stolen Circle Star stock. But now he intended to do it today. If he got there before dark, he could kill two birds with one stone by checking both Lancaster's stock and Howard's stock that had been sold to Lancaster.

But checking the brands on the cattle was not the main reason he was on his way to Lancaster's cow camp. The main reason was the question that was on his mind, the one he wanted very much to ask Lancaster. Was Lancaster's herd exempt, as Howard claimed it was, from supplying beef to the government to hand over to the Cheyenne and Arapaho?

"It could take days to get around to every cow camp on the reservation," Jessie said as she and Brave Buffalo rode beside some grazing cows southeast of Darlington.

"Maybe so a week."

"So far we haven't seen hide nor hair of any Circle Star cattle."

"Men who steal cattle, maybe so they drive them to Kansas."

"I'm beginning to believe that's what happened," Jessie said mournfully. "I feel as Ki does. I can tolerate losing the herd. What I cannot tolerate is the thought of the man or men who killed my drovers escaping justice. If we're unable to track down the Circle Star stock, it's highly likely that we will never know who murdered my men."

They rode on, neither of the speaking, each of them lost in thought. Jessie forced herself to face the fact that she was almost ready to give up the search for the missing Circle Star herd. She had seen and checked the brands today on—how many head of cattle? Hundreds. Not one of them bore her brand. What's more, she had seen no evidence of brand blotting.

Circle Star cattle had been brand-blotted by rustlers before. She recalled the time when Ki had tracked down and captured a small gang of rustlers who had changed the Circle Star brand on the cattle they had stolen by rebranding the animals so that the star within the circle became a second circle. But nothing of the kind had been done this time. At least, not to any cattle she had checked so far.

Perhaps, she thought, Ki will have had better luck than I've had.

They were traveling through a narrow canyon, the walls of which rose tall on either side of them, when they found themselves facing two other riders entering the canyon far ahead of them. The men were driving four head of cattle.

"It's going to be a tight squeeze, getting past those fellows," Jessie said, moving her horse close to the canyon wall on her right.

"Cheyenne," Brave Buffalo said as he rode out in front of her.

Jessie stood up in her stirrups so that she could see above Brave Buffalo. As the two men came closer, she was able to see that her companion had been right. They were Cheyenne Indians.

Moments later, the four bawling beeves they were herding came so close to Jessie that the reek of their bodies filled her nostrils.

Brave Buffalo greeted the two Cheyenne in their language.

Because he had halted and because the canyon was so narrow, Jessie was also obliged to draw rein. She sat her saddle as Brave Buffalo and the two strangers spoke at some length in their native language.

Jessie turned and looked back at the cattle which were no longer moving ahead but standing idly about now that their herders were no longer actively driving them. Her eyes widened in surprise as she recognized the brand the animals wore on their left hips. It was Joe Howard's hay-hook brand. Above it, the original owner's brand had been vented.

She turned her attention to the two Indians who were still talking to Brave Buffalo. As she watched, he pointed to her, then to himself. She wondered what he was saying.

The conversation came to an abrupt end several minutes later. The two Indians rode past Jessie, not bothering to glance in her direction, and began to move their livestock out of the canyon.

"What was that all about?" Jessie asked her companion.

"Those two renegade Cheyenne. They do not stay on reservation. Live wild with their families."

"Those cattle, I believe, they were stolen from a man named Joe Howard."

"That is true. Men say they steal cattle because they cannot find buffalo. They do it many times, they say. This time they take cattle to where they always hide them in big coulee, but other cattle already there so they cannot use coulee."

"Other cattle? You mean other cattle stolen by Indians?"

"Men say many cattle in big coulee. Say it would take from sun to sun to count them. We go to big coulee. See what is there."

"You think my herd might be there along with other cattle?"

"Men say four white men guard cows in coulee," Brave Buffalo said, not answering Jessie's question. "Guards have guns."

Jessie felt excitement surge through her. Her thoughts began to race. No cattle rancher would put cattle in a coulee unless he wanted to make sure they were not seen by others. Which might mean that the cattle were stolen. On the other hand, they might belong to one or more of the men she had been told about who were grazing cattle illegally on the reservation without a signed lease and without paying grass money to the Cheyenne and Arapaho tribal treasuries. Maybe they were hiding the cattle from the Indians. Maybe they grazed them only at night when they were less likely to be seen.

"Where is this coulee?" she asked.

"Not far from here. That way."

Jessie looked in the direction Brave Buffalo had pointed as she rode on beside him. But she saw nothing that would indicate the presence of a coulee anywhere nearby.

She accompanied Brave Buffalo on a circuitous route that led them to the edge of a stretch of land that suddenly gave way to emptiness.

Quietly, they both dismounted and eased up to the edge of the dropoff on hands and knees. Looking down, Jessie found herself staring into the coulee, or ravine, that the two Cheyenne cattle thieves had told Brave Buffalo about. Its sloping sides were covered with thick brush. Its floor was

140

covered with countless head of cattle that were crowded together and kept from escaping by post and pole barriers at each end of the coulee, which extended, Jessie estimated, for nearly two miles.

At each of its ends, two armed guards patrolled the area directly in front of the wooden barriers. They carried rifles. One also had two revolvers in his gunbelt; the three others carried only a single revolver.

Jessie squinted, trying to make out the brands on the cattle below her. She let out a low whistle.

"What do you see?"

"I see some of the Circle Star cattle, that's what I see. I also see some that bear Joe Howard's hayhook brand. All in all, there are six different brands that I can make out. There may be more on the stock down at the far end of the coulee. I also see that they all, as far as I can tell, are marked with a fresh trail brand. When drovers are hired to drive stock that belongs to several different owners, they put a trail brand on all the animals in their charge, which identifies them as part of one herd even though they bear several, or many, different owners' brands."

Jessie shook her head in amazement and emitted another low whistle. "It's a slick set-up. They gather stock they've stolen and trail brand them, and then when they're ready to make their move, they drive them north and sell them in Kansas. Nobody up there is going to ask them any questions. They'll buy the entire lot that they've got to sell and never have any reason to suspect that the cattle have been stolen."

"Do you know those four men?"

"I know two of them by sight. See that hatless one with the black bandanna tied around his head that he's using as a sweat band? And that one down at the other end of the coulee with the red beard?"

"I see them."

"They both work for Chet Lancaster. I saw them in his

cow camp. I don't recognize the other two but my guess is that they also work for Lancaster."

"Then this man, this Lancaster, stole your cattle."

"It certainly does look that way. Now it's up to me to get them back."

"We are going down there?"

"No. I may be headstrong, even hotheaded, as Ki sometimes says I am, but I know better than to try taking on four gunmen with only one man, however willing, to side me. No, we're going to leave and come back with help if we're to go up against that gang down there."

"Where are you going?" Brave Buffalo asked as Jessie got to her feet and headed for the spot where she had left her horse.

"Back to Darlington. I want to meet Ki at the hotel, tell him what we've discovered, and then decide what our next move is going to be."

By the time Ki located Lancaster's main herd that numbered, he estimated, nearly three hundred head, dusk was darkening the land.

If I don't get a move on, he thought, it'll be too dark to see the brands on these beeves. He rode in among the cattle, forcing his horse to shove them aside. Peering at the brands as he went, he made his rough way through the herd.

Before he had finished checking the stock, he spotted a rider heading toward him from the far side of the herd.

He kicked steers out of his way and rode out of the herd just as the rider pulled up and drew both rein and his gun.

Ki stared at the weapon in the man's hand and then at the man himself. "You're fixing to shoot somebody, are you?"

"You maybe," the rider snarled. "That's what we do with rustlers. We shoot them."

"I'm not a rustler."

"Is that a fact now? You were just paying a social call on those cattle I caught you riding in the middle of, is that it?"

Ki hesitated, not wanting to tell the rider his real reason for riding in among the herd in case the man subsequently reported his investigative presence to Lancaster and the cattleman took offense and held the matter against Jessie.

"What's the matter, the cat got your tongue?" When Ki said nothing, the man continued, "No matter. I caught you red-handed trying to cut cows from Mr. Lancaster's herd. Now we're going to go see the boss and let him decide what's to be done with you. Move out, mister!"

Ki obeyed his barked order.

The two men rode north in silence as dusk deepened into darkness. They arrived at Lancaster's cow camp twenty minutes later.

Lancaster's rider called out, "Got ourselves a cow thief, boss!"

Lancaster, who had been standing by the fire with his men, turned at the sound of the shout. "What's all this about, Ki?"

"You know this here jasper, boss?" asked the startled rider.

"I know him. What seems to be the problem?"

"I caught him riding right smack in the middle of our main herd. He was trying to cut some cows out of it."

"That's not altogether true, Mr. Lancaster," Ki said quietly. "I was in the middle of your herd. But that's because I got caught up in a mill. I was working my way out of it when this man here rode up, threw down on me, and accused me of trying to steal some of your stock."

"It's all right," Lancaster told his rider. "This man is a friend of Miss Starbuck's. I'm sure he wouldn't steal cattle. You made an honest mistake."

The rider glowered at Ki for a moment and then said, "No offense meant, mister."

"None taken," Ki replied mildly, glad that the lie he had told Lancaster about having been caught in a mill had been believed.

When the rider had gone, Lancaster said, "You're out late, Ki."

"Yes, sir, I am. I've been trying to find our missing herd. Jessie has been doing the same south of here. I should tell you that, although we haven't found the herd, we did find its drovers." Ki told Lancaster what had happened to Statler and his men.

When he had done so, Lancaster shook his head. "I'm sorry to hear that, Ki. I never for a moment thought they'd been killed. I know this is rough country but the Indians never got that far out of line before. It's a terrible thing that they did. A truly terrible thing."

"It was that," Ki agreed, his mind racing as he plotted a strategy, which he then promptly proceeded to pursue with Lancaster. "The loss of the herd is a substantial one for Starbuck Enterprises," he said. "It, together with the cattle we've been losing through theft and confiscation is beginning to take a toll on Jessie's profit margin.

"Which reminds me. I was talking to Joe Howard earlier today and he tells me he's fed up with what's been going on here on the leased lands. He told me he's thrown in the towel and sold out to you."

"Yes, that's so."

"Howard also told me that you've been a lucky man."

"Lucky? How so?"

"Howard said you haven't lost a single steer to the cavalry, which has the bad habit, I understand, of confiscating cattle—taking them from men like yourself—and turning them over to the Indians at the agency."

Did Lancaster's eyes narrow? Ki wasn't sure.

"Howard is mistaken."

"He is?"

"Like others on the leased lands, I've lost a number of

cattle to the army despite my very vociferous protests, which to date, I regret to say, have been unavailing."

"Then, despite what Howard said, you too are a member of the cattle-losers' club out here?"

"A member, I might say, in very good standing. I have lost a total of fifty-four head on three separate occasions during March and April of this year."

Ki nodded, yawned. "Well, sir, I think it's time I called it a night. I'll be leaving now and heading back to Darlington."

"Give Miss Starbuck my regards, will you? And tell her I was heartily sorry to hear the awful news about her drovers. I hope she will at least be fortunate enough to find her missing cattle alive and well."

Ki found Jessie impatiently pacing the lobby of the Murray Hotel when he arrived there just after nine o'clock that night.

She hurried up to him. "I found the herd!" she announced.

"You found them? Where?"

"Before I answer your question—are you hungry? I'm starved. I haven't eaten, but I didn't want to leave here and miss you so I waited for you to show up. Let's go and have some supper." Jessie took Ki's arm and practically rushed him out the door.

After they had placed their orders at a restaurant two doors down from the hotel that had been about to close when they arrived, Jessie leaned forward across the table and said, "Brave Buffalo and I were out hunting for the herd when we ran into two Cheyenne Indians who had four steers with them. Brave Buffalo talked to them. As it turned out, they weren't reservation Indians, and the steers they had with them they had stolen from Joe Howard. They bore his hayhook brand."

Jessie quickly told Ki the rest of the story—about her

trip with Brave Buffalo to the coulee where the cattle were hidden, about seeing Circle Star stock among them, and about recognizing two of the four men guarding the coulee as Lancaster employees.

"So it's clear to me at this point," she continued, "that Lancaster not only stole my herd but also murdered Statler and the others. Lancaster has also been stealing, apparently systematically, cattle from the people leasing grazing land here in the Territory. I saw quite a number of different brands on the beeves in that coulee."

"It's hard to believe," Ki said and then fell silent as the waiter placed the food they had ordered in front of them.

"What is?" Jessie asked when the waiter had gone.

"That Lancaster stole the Circle Star cattle and murdered the drovers. By the way, I just came from talking to him."

"What did he have to say?" Jessie cut a piece from her steak and ate it.

"An interesting thing or two. I went to see him after talking to Joe Howard. By the way, Howard is throwing in the towel. He has sublet his land to Lancaster, he told me, and doesn't intend to use it himself any more. He also said—and this I found very interesting—that he thought the Indian agent, Amos Butler, was up to no good. Howard suspects Butler of having a hand in seeing to it that people who have cattle requisitioned by the Fourth Cavalry for distribution to the Indians don't get paid. He suggested to me that he thought Lancaster might also have something to do with his bad luck."

"What makes him think that? Did he have proof when you spoke to him that Lancaster had stolen some of his cattle?"

"No, he didn't. He didn't even suspect Lancaster of stealing his stock. He blamed his losses on the Indians. The reason he was down on Lancaster was due to the fact that he claimed Lancaster had never had any cattle confiscated by the army for the Indians. He thought that was odd."

"Come to think of it, so do I."

"But Howard was wrong about that matter."

"What do you mean?" Jessie asked. She summoned the waiter and ordered tea for Ki and coffee for herself.

"I told Lancaster that Howard said he was the only lessee out here who hadn't had stock taken from him to feed the Indians. He insisted that Howard was mistaken on that point. He told me he had lost cattle to the army on three different occasions during March and April, fifty-four head in all, he said."

"He's going to lose more than cattle by the time I'm through with him," Jessie said sharply. "He's going to lose his life at the end of a hangman's noose for murdering those men."

"What are you planning to do next?"

"I'm not exactly sure. I wanted to talk things over with you first. But I do have an idea or two."

"I'd like to hear them."

"First of all, I think we should go to the agency and tell Butler what we've found out about Lancaster—that he's a cattle thief and a killer. Then I think we should go to Fort Reno and get Major Lane to lend us some troopers for support when we confront Lancaster with what we've found out about him. We certainly can't take him alone, just the two of us. Not with all his men backing him up. But I'd be willing to try even that if it became necessary."

"Lancaster will put up a fight, we can be certain of that," Ki commented, as the waiter returned with their coffee and tea. "We'll need all the support we can muster if we're to take him down without getting hurt—or worse—in the process."

"I'm sure Major Lane will cooperate with us, given the circumstances."

"I'm looking forward to tomorrow," Ki said as he

sipped his tea. "I have a question or two for Amos Butler that I've been itching to ask him ever since I talked to Lancaster this evening."

"We'll go to the agency first thing in the morning," Jessie said, "if that's all right with you."

"Normally, I'd say it isn't. I'm no fan of your dawn jaunts, as you well know, Jessie. But for this purpose, first thing in the morning is fine with me."

★
Chapter 10

After a hurried breakfast of flapjacks and coffee, Jessie and Ki left for the Darlington Agency before the new day's sun was an hour old.

When they arrived at their destination, Jessie said, "Look, there's Brave Buffalo. He told me he would meet me here when we parted yesterday."

"Why did he want to meet you?" Ki inquired as Brave Buffalo stepped down from the porch of the building that housed the agency and came toward them.

"He wanted to clear, or partially clear, at any rate, the Indians in this matter of stock-stealing."

As they drew rein and dismounted, Brave Buffalo greeted them with a nod.

"Have you seen Mr. Butler?" Jessie asked him as Ki looped the reins of their horses around the hitchrail in front of the building.

"No."

Jessie went up on the porch and knocked on the door. When no one answered it, she knocked again, louder this time. When still no one answered her knock, she called Butler's name and then knocked on the door a third time.

A few moments later, Butler's head popped out of a second story window. The tassel on the man's flannel nightcap kept swinging back and forth in front of his bleary eyes as he stared sleepily down at them.

"Who's there?" he called out in a ragged voice.

"Jessica Starbuck."

"My dear Miss Starbuck," an aggrieved Butler declared, looking up at the brightening sky, "it is just past dawn. I have been in bed—"

"Mr. Butler, I'm sorry to bother you at this early hour, and I would not have done so were it not for the fact that I am here on a very important matter and must discuss it with you now."

"What can possibly be so important," Butler asked, an indignant edge creeping into his tone, "that you must rouse a man from his bed at this unseemly hour of the morning?"

"Murder, Mr. Butler."

Butler's eyes and mouth popped open. He silently mouthed the word "murder" that Jessie had just spoken. He brushed the tassel of his nightcap away from in front of his face and blinked down at them. "Oh, my. I shall be right down. Give me a moment to dress. Oh, my. Murder you say?"

"Yes, murder," Jessie repeated.

Butler withdrew his head from the window.

Jessie stood on the porch, impatiently tapping her toe on the wooden floor, her arms folded across her chest.

When the front door finally opened, she turned and strode into the building past Butler, followed by Ki and Brave Buffalo.

"Sit down, Miss Starbuck," Butler said, pulling his braces up over his shoulders. "Do forgive my appearance. I didn't have time to dress properly. I couldn't find my spectacles at first, and I had the devil's own time trying to button my braces without them."

Jessie remained standing. "Mr. Butler, I have discovered that one of the men you lease reservation land to—"

"I beg your pardon, Miss Starbuck. Let me make one thing clear. *I* don't lease the land. The Cheyenne and Arapaho *tribes* lease it. I merely oversee and approve the arrangement to be sure that they are in the Indians' best interests."

"Mr. Butler," Jessie continued, "I'm convinced that one of the lessees is not only a cattle thief but also a murderer."

"I trust I'm not intruding."

The voice had come from the second floor landing.

Jessie and the others looked up to find Mark Demming, Butler's assistant, standing there and gazing down at them, a benign expression of his bemused face. Without waiting for a response from any of the people looking up at him, he descended the stairs and joined them. "Good morning, Miss Starbuck." He nodded a greeting to Ki and Brave Buffalo.

"Mark, Miss Starbuck tells me there is a murderer among us!" Butler exclaimed, pushing his spectacles up on his nose.

"A murderer? Who might that be, Miss Starbuck?"

"The man's name is Chet Lancaster," Jessie stated flatly. "He is also a cattle thief."

"I don't believe it," Demming said. "Mr. Lancaster is a fine upstanding gentleman. I *won't* believe it."

"Believe it or not as you will, Mr. Demming," Jessie persisted. "What I have told you is the truth. I can prove the charges I'm making, both of them."

"We have found Miss Starbuck's missing cattle," Ki offered. "We found them hidden in a coulee along with cattle bearing other owners' brands and guarded by four men, two of whom Miss Starbuck identifies as employees of Mr. Lancaster."

Demming glared at him. "Who, sir, might you be?"

"I'm a friend of Miss Starbuck's. My name is Ki."

"We found the herd in the coulee Ki mentioned," Jessie said and then described the ravine's location.

"I come here," Brave Buffalo said to the two agents, "to tell you not only Indians steal white man's cattle. White men steal cattle too. Maybe so next time cattle is missing you not be so quick to say Brave Buffalo and his Dog Soldiers steal cattle. I tell you many times. Dog Soldiers do not steal cattle. We will starve before we take white man's cattle for food."

"I intend to go over to Fort Reno," Jessie told the agents, "and enlist the aid of the army to help me and Ki apprehend Lancaster and any of his men who may have had a hand in the murder of the drovers who worked for me."

"Surely, Miss Starbuck," a suddenly ashen-faced Butler said, "you don't mean to tell me that Mr. Lancaster killed the men who were in charge of that herd of cattle you came here to inquire about?"

"That is exactly what I mean to tell you, Mr. Butler."

"You have found the missing men then?"

"I found them," Ki replied. "They had been murdered, shot to death with both bullets and arrows."

"Then surely Indians must have murdered them," Demming declared firmly.

"Not so," Brave Buffalo said.

"But you said they had been shot with arrows," Demming pointed out.

Jessie quickly explained why the arrows would not have been made by either the Cheyenne or the Arapaho.

"White men make those arrows," Brave Buffalo said. "They do it to make it look like Indians killed drovers. But lady say truth. Cheyenne and Arapaho not use crow feathers on arrows. Crow is sacred bird of both tribes. White men make arrows to make trouble over murders for Indians."

"I do believe Brave Buffalo is right," Butler said to Demming. "It was a trick played by someone who did not know about the sanctity of the relationship of the Indians to the crow."

"Not so fast," Demming cautioned. "It could well be that some renegade Indians used the crow feathers so that

152

suspicion would be turned upon white men and not Indians. A kind of trick within a trick, if you see my point."

"I suppose that is possible," Butler speculated.

Demming stroked his red mustache, a complacent look in his pale blue eyes.

"No," Brave Buffalo said. "Arrows made by white men. Bad work. No Indian make such bad arrows."

"There's another point to consider in all this," Jessie said. "What motive would Indians have for killing my drovers?"

"To take possession of your cattle obviously," a smug Demming answered.

Jessie smiled.

It took a moment for the assistant agent to realize why she was smiling. "I see," he said not at all smugly. "If the Indians had killed the drovers to take possession of their cattle—"

"The cattle would not now be in a coulee guarded by Chet Lancaster's men," Jessie argued.

"Perhaps Mr. Lancaster's men took the cattle away from the Indians," Demming offered lamely.

"If he had done that," Ki said, "why didn't he return the Circle Star stock to Jeff Marsden who is in charge of the range leased by Starbuck Enterprises?"

"And what about all the other owners' cattle I saw in the coulee?" Jessie asked. "The ones bearing the brands of other owners besides myself. How do you account for their presence in the coulee?"

When Demming remained silent, Ki said, addressing Butler this time, "There's another matter I've been meaning to bring up. I'll put it in the form of a question, if I may. How many times have you gentlemen obtained cattle from Lancaster to give to the Indians here on the reservation?"

"I really don't know to be perfectly honest about it," Butler admitted. "As I told Miss Starbuck when she was here the first time, I do not handle the accounting for this office. Mr. Demming does."

"Then maybe you can answer my question for me," Ki said, turning expectantly to Demming.

"Why, yes, I do believe I can. I shall consult my ledger and find out that information for you."

"Do it, Mr. Demming," Ki said and then added, as if he had had an afterthought, "if you don't mind."

Demming turned and left the room.

As soon as he had gone, Ki asked Butler another question. "Who keeps the records of payments made by the government to the owners of the cattle taken to feed the Indians. Would that also be Demming?"

Butler nodded. "Why do you ask?"

"Excuse me a moment." Ki hurriedly left the room. In the hall, he looked both ways, and when he saw an open door on his left, he headed for it. He stood in its doorway and watched silently as Demming, with his back to the door, hastily made notations in a large green ledger.

A moment later, Demming picked up the open ledger and waved it about to dry the fresh ink on its pages. Then he snapped it shut and turned. When he saw Ki watching him, he halted.

"What was that you just wrote in your ledger, Mr. Demming?" Ki asked.

"Why, nothing. Nothing important, that is. Entries I failed to make earlier."

"Would those entries you forgot to make earlier have anything to do with Lancaster by any chance?"

"Why, uh, yes, as a matter of fact they did."

"What a coincidence," Ki marveled. "May I see them?"

"See them?"

"The entries you just made." Ki held out his hand for the ledger.

Demming clutched it tightly against his chest. "The

matters recorded here are private, sir. They are not made available to the general public."

"Oh, I understand all that, Demming. But then, you see, I'm not the general public. I mean I'm representing the interests of one of the reservation's lessees, Starbuck Enterprises. Let's see that ledger. If you're not of a mind to hand it over, I think I should tell you straight out that I'm of a mind to take it from you."

Demming swallowed twice, his Adam's apple bobbing. He looked about the room as if seeking a way to escape from it. Without looking directly at Ki but off to one side, he held out the ledger.

Ki took it from him and began to leaf through its pages.

Demming started for the door.

Ki stepped to the side to prevent him from leaving the room. "I might just have a question or two for you once I'm through with this ledger. So don't go."

"You have absolutely no right to—"

"Demming."

"What?"

"Shut up!"

"I say, what is going on here?"

Ki looked up at Butler who had just spoken as he bustled his way into the room and at Jessie and Brave Buffalo who were standing in the doorway.

"Mr. Demming and I are having a chat about the agency records," Ki answered Butler as he flipped through more pages. "Ah, here's what I've been looking for. Demming was making a few entries when I got here. He was in such a hurry to do so that he didn't wait for the ink he was using to dry thoroughly. See here where it's smeared?"

Butler peered through his spectacles at the page Ki was displaying for his benefit. "I see, yes, I most surely do see."

"Then you see that the entries Demming was just making have to do with the number of cattle taken from Lancaster's herd and the dates on which they were taken."

"Yes, but what—"

"Amos, I really think this man had gone too far," Demming protested. "He practically seized that ledger from me, and I respectfully submit to you that he has no right to it or to the information it contains."

"I'm afraid I must agree with my colleague, Ki," Butler said in an apologetic tone. "That ledger contains privileged information."

"I'm not usually one to pry," Ki said evenly, "but I'm very much interested in this matter. First of all, I think it's strange that Demming made these entries only after I expressed an interest in knowing how many, if any, of Lancaster's cattle wound up in the bellies of your Indians. Second of all, I think it's even stranger that what Demming wrote in this ledger just now concerning the matter doesn't match what Lancaster himself told me when I questioned him about the subject only yesterday."

"I'm afraid I'm not following you, sir," Butler declared. "What is he talking about, Mark?"

"I haven't the slightest idea, Amos."

"Let me explain," Ki offered. "It says here—Demming just wrote down here—that ten head of cattle were taken from Lancaster by the army on March 5th of this year. It then says fifteen more head were taken on April 2nd."

"So?" prompted Butler, fussing with his spectacles.

"So, Mr. Butler," Ki continued, "Lancaster told me he had lost fifty-four head on three separate occasions during March and April."

"I see," Butler said thoughtfully with a glance at Demming. "A discrepancy, clearly."

"I haven't had time recently to make all the entries that would keep my ledger up to date," Demming explained.

Butler looked at Ki, obviously satisfied with his assistant's explanation.

"There's another thing of interest in this ledger, Mr.

156

Butler," Ki said. "Look here." He flipped to another page and pointed to a list of entries. "Listed here, under accounts receivable, are the amounts of money received—and when each was received—from the government in payment for the cattle taken from your lessees and given to the Indians."

"I can see that."

"Now look here, if you will. There are no entries at all under the accounts payable side of the page for the past three months—March, April, and May. Which makes me wonder where the money received went."

"Why, it must still be in our safe," Butler suggested, heading for the locked iron safe that sat on the floor in a corner of the room.

"Don't do that!" Demming cried. Then, more calmly, "The money, I had to use it to buy staples to distribute to the Indians. But I intended to pay the cattle owners once there were sufficient funds—"

"You're a liar, Demming!" Ki accused. "Now what I want to know is this. Who got the money? You?"

"Of course not. I just told you that!"

Ki put down the ledger, stepped forward, and seized a fistful of Demming's shirt, practically lifting the man off the floor as he did so. "What did you really do with the money?"

When Demming didn't answer, Ki slammed him up against the wall.

"Stop that!" Butler cried and was about to intervene, but Jessie reached out, took his arm, and prevented him from doing so.

Ki's left fist flew. It landed in Demming's solar plexus, doubling the man over and causing him to gasp. Ki immediately jerked him upright and drew back his fist again.

"No!" Demming shrieked, his eyes wide with fright. "Don't hit me again!"

"Tell me," Ki said simply, keeping his fist poised.

"Miss Starbuck," Butler exclaimed, shaking himself free of Jessie, "surely you cannot countenance this disgraceful behavior on the part of your friend!"

"I kept the money for myself!" Demming gasped, his alarmed eyes on Ki's fist. "I blamed the agency's failure to pay the money owed the cattlemen on the government's failure to send us the money due."

"Didn't you know that someone would catch up with you sooner or later?" an incredulous Jessie asked, with a pointed glance in Butler's direction.

"I was going to get out," Demming said. "Leave here before anyone found out."

"Mark," a shocked Butler cried, "I trusted you. I treated you as if you were my own son. How could you have done this to me—to everyone involved?"

"How?" Demming snarled. "It was easy. You paid little or no attention to the agency records. As long as no one bothered you unduly, you were perfectly content to let me handle things. You were far more interested in making trips to Washington and to the Central Superintendency in Kansas to talk to anyone who would listen to you about the plight of the noble Red Man. Well, I say, may the noble Red Man be damned!"

As Brave Buffalo made an aggressive move in Demming's direction, Jessie restrained him as she had restrained Butler earlier and whispered something in his ear.

A shocked Butler stared speechlessly at his assistant.

Ki released his hold on Demming. "You never ordered the army to take any of Lancaster's cattle, did you?"

"No."

"What did Lancaster do—pay you to keep his herd intact?"

"Two hundred dollars a month."

Ki turned to Jessie. "If Lancaster hadn't lied to me last night about having had cattle taken from him by the army, I never would have suspected what was going on here. On the one hand, Howard had told me that Lancaster's herd was and had been untouched. So I decided to check out Howard's claim with Lancaster who, as you know, then lied to me to divert suspicion from himself and, incidentally, from his colleague, Demming, here. The way I figure it, Lancaster still made money even though he was paying Demming two hundred dollars a month to leave his herd alone. He would realize more money from the sale of his beeves in Dodge than he would have gotten from the government if it had confiscated them. It was an arrangement that suited both men just fine."

"Well, it doesn't suit me fine!" Butler suddenly thundered. "Demming, I want you out of here right now. You're through. Dismissed! Do you hear me?"

"I hear you. Now, you hear me. You're as much to blame for what has happened here as I am. If you had paid closer attention—indeed, any attention, by God—to the day-by-day operation of this benighted agency, I would never have been able to get away with what I did. That ought to give you one or two sleepless nights in the future.

"And, let me tell you, I got away with plenty! Do you remember complaining about the stringy beef we bought from the cattle contractor who was doing business with us last month? Well, I paid him half the going price for that nearly worthless meat but entered the *full* price in our records. I pocketed half the money from that transaction, and it was only one of many such transactions over the past several months."

"I never knew!" a stricken Butler moaned.

"You *should* have known!" Demming shouted at him. "If you were half the go-getter that I was—if you cared half as much about the Indians as I cared about making money—you damn well *would* have known!"

Jessie and Brave Buffalo stepped aside to allow Demming to stalk from the room.

Butler collapsed in a chair, supporting his bowed head

in his hands. "He's right, you know," he said in a low voice. "I should have paid more attention to things. I should have made it my business—it *was* my business to know what was going on here, to know what Demming was doing."

He looked forlornly up at Jessie. "But you see I thought that if I lobbied important people—at the Central Superintendency, for example—on behalf of the Indians I would be doing more good than by attending to what I considered at the time to be little more than mundane clerical matters of far less import."

"Mr. Butler," Jessie said, "you did what you thought was the right thing to do. No one can fault you for that."

"You had no reason to suspect Demming of corruption," Ki pointed out.

"You mustn't condemn yourself," Jessie said, "for what has happened. The thing to do now is to rectify matters as best you can and to go on from here."

"You're very kind, Miss Starbuck," Butler said gratefully. "You are also right. I will go on, and this time, I will do better. I'm sure I shall."

Jessie heard the note of self-doubt in Butler's voice. "I know you will," she told the agent with conviction in an effort to drown out that note of self-doubt.

Butler rose. "Thank you, Ki, for exposing Demming's corruption. I appreciate it despite the shock the revelation has caused me."

Ki shook hands with Butler and then left the building with Jessie and Brave Buffalo.

Once outside, he said, "I suppose Fort Reno is our next stop."

"Yes, it is," Jessie said. "Brave Buffalo, are you coming with us?"

The Cheyenne shook his head. "I have much to do here at agency. You not need Brave Buffalo. You and pony soldiers can fight Lancaster. If I help you fight him, people

160

say Cheyenne Indians on warpath again. Make much trouble for us."

"I understand," Jessie said.

Later, as she and Ki rode southwest toward the North Fork of the Canadian River, she smiled to herself.

Ki gave her a questioning look.

"I was thinking about what Brave Buffalo just said," she offered in response to Ki's look. "The Cheyenne may not be setting out on the warpath. But we sure are, aren't we?"

It was Ki's turn to smile.

They forded the Canadian and shortly thereafter arrived at Fort Reno, which consisted of a haphazard cluster of buildings built of planks and roofed with canvas. On the fort's northern perimeter were several neat rows of canvas tents.

They rode up to the doorless building that bore a sign above its entrance that said: COMMANDANT'S QUARTERS.

Leaving their horses ground-hitched outside the building, they went inside and found a corporal seated behind a desk.

"May I help you?" he asked them politely.

"We'd like to see Major Lane," Jessie responded as politely.

"I'll see if he's available." The corporal rose and went through a door behind his desk.

Jessie and Ki waited. In a moment, the corporal reappeared and said, "Major Lane will see you now."

Once inside the major's office, Jessie introduced herself and Ki.

Major Lane, a gray-haired man with an air of elegance about him, acknowledged the introductions with a half-bow and asked, "How may I be of service?"

Jessie explained that she had come to request help in apprehending Chet Lancaster whom she accused of murdering her drovers and stealing her cattle along with cattle belonging to others who were leasing land on the reservation.

When she had finished speaking, Major Lane pursed his lips, cleared his throat, and said, "I'm afraid I can be of no help to you, Miss Starbuck, much as I would like to be."

"Why not, Major?" Ki asked.

"The matter Miss Starbuck has just described to me is not within the military's jurisdiction. It is strictly a civilian affair and should, therefore, be handled by the civil authorities."

"What civil authorities?" an annoyed Ki asked. "The courts in Kansas? That could take weeks—months."

Unruffled, Major Lane replied, "As you may or may not know, the Cheyenne and Arapaho reservation is within the jurisdiction of the federal court based in Fort Smith, Arkansas, over which Judge Isaac Parker presides. That court employs a number of deputy marshals deployed throughout Indian Territory. It is to one or more of those law officers that you should present your problem. I'm sorry I can do nothing for you. I appreciate the seriousness of the matter that concerns you, but I can only wish you good luck in bringing it to a successful conclusion."

Jessie looked at Ki and saw the disappointment on his face, which, she suspected, probably mirrored her own expression. She thanked Major Lane for taking the time to see them and for listening to what she had to say, and then she left the building with Ki at her side.

She drew a deep breath as she picked up her horse's reins and lifted them over the animal's head. She drew another deep breath as she stepped into the saddle.

"We could try to find one of those deputy marshals the major mentioned," Ki proposed.

"I didn't give them serious thought when I was making plans to take Lancaster," Jessie said. "They're spread thin throughout Indian Territory. Few of them, in actual practice, get farther west than the Katy Railroad. Even if we were to locate one of the marshals and he agreed to help us, that would still leave us with three on our side against Lancaster and all his men."

"Not the best of odds."

"Decidedly not. But I'm determined to see to it that Lancaster pays for what he has done, and if that means I have to bring him down alone, then that's what I'll do."

"Jessie, you're not alone."

"I know that. I didn't mean to exclude you, Ki. It was just that I spoke sloppily. I know I can always depend on you to help me when the going gets rough."

"As it is right now."

They rode on and were almost at the boundary of the fort's grounds when Jessie said, "There's Lieutenant Stowe."

"Where?"

"He just stepped behind that tent over there."

Stowe reappeared from behind the tent, and when he noticed Jessie and Ki, he smiled.

Jessie and Ki both drew rein as he hurried over to them.

"Good morning, Miss Starbuck, Ki," he said pleasantly, touching the brim of his campaign hat to Jessie. "What brings you here to the fort?"

"We came to enlist the aid of some of your troopers, Lieutenant, but our mission has been, I'm sorry to say, unsuccessful."

"Your mission?"

"We came here to ask the military to help us apprehend Chet Lancaster at his cow camp and then take the four men he's got guarding the stock he stole from me and other cattle owners."

"You've located your missing cattle?"

"I have. And Ki found our drovers who had been murdered by Lancaster." Jessie proceeded to tell Stowe about Ki's discovery of the dead drovers and then about her and

Brave Buffalo having found the missing cattle hidden in a coulee.

"I never knew there was such a coulee on the reservation. Where is it located?"

Jessie told him.

"I'm sorry that the army couldn't lend you a hand," Stowe said.

"We need more than a hand," Ki said. "We need a lot of hands and also a lot of guns."

"But it appears we're not going to get them from the army," Jessie remarked. A thought suddenly occured to her. "Unless, that is, you and the men under your command would be willing to help us take Lancaster into custody, Lieutenant."

"Me? Oh, I couldn't do that, Miss Starbuck. If Major Lane were ever to find out that I had interfered in a civilian dispute, he'd skin me alive."

The hope that had so suddenly flared in Jessie just as suddenly died.

"I'm sorry," Stowe said. "I know that doesn't help but—"

"No, it certainly doesn't," Jessie said. "But I do appreciate your sentiments nevertheless. Good day to you."

"You cut him kind of short," Ki observed as he and Jessie rode toward the river.

"I was angry with him," Jessie explained. "As I'm also angry with Major Lane. What good does it do to have an army out here trying to keep the peace when they won't help when murder and theft has been committed?"

"You're being foolish, Jessie, and I can understand why. You're upset, rightfully so, over what has happened. But don't take your anger out on the army. They can't step into the middle of a non-military matter. If we want the law on our side, we'll just have to find ourselves a deputy marshal from Fort Smith to help us as Major Lane recommended.

But we've already agreed that there's little likelihood of our being able to do that."

"You're right. I should have held my tongue. Lieutenant Stowe could do or say nothing other than what he did."

"Nice looking fellow, the Lieutenant," Ki commented as they forded the Canadian River.

Jessie looked at him.

He raised his eyebrows in an expression of utter innocence.

They rode on, and as they were passing the Darlington Agency, Ki said, "That looks like Brave Buffalo standing over there by the sawmill."

Jessie looked in the direction Ki was pointing. "It is him." She waved. "He doesn't see us."

Neither Jessie nor Ki, as they continued heading west, saw Brave Buffalo turn, notice them, and stand watching as they rode away, a frown on his dark face.

★
Chapter 11

As they neared the site of Lancaster's cow camp, Jessie suggested to Ki that they dismount and move in on foot to scout the area.

"That way," she said, "we can find out how many men Lancaster has with him in camp, whether or not they're all armed, and what our chances are of taking Lancaster prisoner."

"We can leave our horses over there," Ki said, indicating a grove of blackjack oaks. "Then we can take cover on the camp's western perimeter—up there where that limestone ridge will shield us from anybody on its other side."

They turned their horses and did as Ki had suggested. Leaving their mounts hidden among the blackjack oaks, they made their way across an open stretch of sandy land until they reached the bottom of the ridge.

Jessie drew her Colt as they silently made their way up to the crest of the ridge where they flattened themselves on the ground and looked down at the two men gathered around a cook fire below.

"Look!" Jessie whispered to Ki. "That's Demming down there with Lancaster."

"I bet you I can tell you what he's doing here."

"He must have come to warn Lancaster that we intended to try to enlist the cavalry to help us capture his partner in corruption."

"That would be my guess. Honor among thieves, or some such thing."

"Lancaster's men must be out working his cattle—those that aren't stationed at the coulee with the stolen stock."

"But they might not be much longer. Not now that Demming has arrived to warn Lancaster that we're coming for him."

"I'd say now is the time to make our move. Before those two are backed up by reinforcements. Luck's on our side. It's two against two and, as far as I can tell, Demming isn't armed, which turns the tables in our favor."

"Demming could be packing a hideout gun," Ki cautioned. "He's the kind of slippery snake who would be liable to do just that."

"How do you want to handle this?"

"One of us can go in from the front and face up to Lancaster. The other one can skirt around the north side of this ridge and then move down into those trees over there by that stream and come in from behind as a backup in case any shooting starts."

"I'll go in from the front," Jessie announced.

"It would be safer for you if you played backup and I went in for a face-to-face meeting with Lancaster."

"No, I want to confront him. I want to see his face when I tell him we've found out about what he did. For that I'm willing to take the risk."

Ki knew better than to argue with Jessie. He also understood her desire to want to confront Lancaster with her knowledge of his crimes. He therefore raised no objection to the plan she had proposed but said instead, "Give me five minutes to get down off this ridge and into those trees behind Lancaster and Demming. Then you make your move. All right?"

"That's fine with me."

Ki slid down below the crest of the ridge and then got to

his feet and went running, his body bent to avoid skylining himself.

When he disappeared from sight, Jessie suddenly felt very much alone. The hair on her scalp prickled as she continued watching Lancaster, the man who had killed her drovers and who would, she knew, kill her as well without a pang of guilt or remorse. The fear that had started to sidle through her was suddenly swept away when an image of young Billy MacKenzie appeared in her mind's eye, lying dead, his body rotting. This horror was the doing of the rapacious cattleman she was now so intently watching, and so intensely hating.

She forced herself to wait where she was for another several minutes. Then, gun firmly in hand, she rose and boldly strode down the slope toward the two men below.

Demming was the first to spot her.

"Here she comes!" he cried, pointing at her.

Lancaster turned quickly, saw her, smiled. "Well, well, if it isn't the lovely Miss Starbuck. I have no need to ask you why you've come here. I know that, thanks to Mr. Demming who has kept me faithfully informed concerning recent developments at the Indian agency. I know, for example, that you have discovered the profitable arrangement that has existed for some time between Demming and myself."

"Did Demming also tell you that I discovered the whereabouts of my missing cattle and that I identified at least two of the men guarding them and the other stock you stole as your employees?"

"Yes, he did."

"How many of your men participated in the killing of my drovers and the hiding of their bodies in the gorge where Ki found them?"

"How many? Why, all fifteen of them, including the four you saw at the coulee. Each of them has been carefully chosen by me, and I modestly add that each one is fiercely loyal to me. Their loyalty, I must admit, has its roots in the generous salaries and bonuses I pay them, but I hasten to add that it is loyalty nonetheless, whatever motivates it.

"Hold on one moment, Miss Starbuck," Lancaster continued. "Before you say anything else, let me mention to you that Demming told me you intended to arrive here backed by the force of the United States Army. Was he mistaken? I see no cavalry. Or have you hidden them in the bushes back there along the trail somewhere?"

Jessie raged inwardly at Lancaster's mocking tone, at the way he was openly sneering at her. But she forced herself to remain calm. "I don't need the army to deal with you. Get on your horse, Lancaster. We're riding out of here."

The cattleman merely smirked. "I take it you want to join your drovers in death. Otherwise you would not have come here with one gun against two men, one of them—I refer to myself—armed as you are."

"If there's any dying to be done here today," Jessie said, "it's you who'll be doing it, Lancaster. That's a promise."

"Is it one you think you can keep?"

"You might try to drop me. You might even manage to do it. But I'll take one—maybe both—of you down with me. Think about it. Then think about something else. I may not be playing all my cards up front. I might have a card up my sleeve. An ace."

"You're talking about your friend, Ki, I assume," a smug Lancaster replied.

"She is," Ki said as he emerged from the trees and took up a position only two yards behind the two men who were now positioned between Jessie and him.

"One man is a poor substitute for cavalry, Miss Starbuck," Lancaster commented suavely without turning in Ki's direction.

"One *unarmed* man," Demming simpered. "The half-blood doesn't even have a gun!"

"Speaking of guns," Lancaster said, "reminds me of what I wanted to say to you, Miss Starbuck, that there really need be no violence between us. You suggested a moment ago that you had an ace up your sleeve, and lo and behold so you did. Well, I too have an ace, and it is this. In order not to put too fine a point on it, let me call it a business proposition."

"I would never do business with you, Lancaster," Jessie said firmly.

"Please. First hear me out before you turn me down. You know now or at least you must suspect what I have been doing here on the reservation. Not just leasing land for my own use. No. I have also been systematically increasing the size of my holdings by—"

"By driving out other cattle owners like Joe Howard," Ki interrupted. "By stealing their stock and blaming the thefts on the Indians. By getting Demming to bleed their herds dry to feed the Indians. And, I'm willing to wager at this point, by poisoning their stock with arsenic to further damage the cattle owners and encourage them to give up their leased land as Howard did."

"All quite true except for one point," Lancaster admitted. "Not all the stock Demming arranged for the army to confiscate from Howard and others went to feed the Indians. Much more of it found its way in secret to the railheads in Kansas where it was sold for a sizable profit."

"A profit that I pocketed," Demming openly boasted.

Ki muttered a colorful oath.

Jessie was barely able to restrain herself from doing the same thing.

"Now, as I was saying before being so rudely interrupted," Lancaster resumed, "I want to suggest to you, Miss Starbuck, that we join forces instead of fighting one another. That we set out to become the joint lessees of all the land available for leasing here on the reservation. We can count on the continuing cooperation of Demming in our venture, which will help to insure the profitability of such an undertaking."

Jessie, barely able to believe her ears, said, "What about Amos Butler? He knows now what you two have been doing—most of it, anyway."

"I intend to see to it that Butler has an accident—a fatal one. Perhaps he will be shot by an unknown assailant for some unknown reason. Perhaps he will die in a fall from a horse. Something can be easily arranged."

"Then I will be appointed to take control of the Darlington Agency," Demming interjected with obvious glee.

"What if I don't agree to your proposal?" Jessie asked, suspecting that she already knew the answer to her question.

"In that regrettable case," Lancaster said smoothly, "you and your friend, Ki, will die."

"You're going to kill us?" an incredulous Jessie asked. "Your gun is still leathered; mine's already in my hand. Demming isn't armed. Ki is."

"She's bluffing, Lancaster," Demming said. "The half-blood doesn't have a gun any more than I do."

"Miss Starbuck," Lancaster said in a tone a teacher might take with a child who is slow to learn, "as you know, I've been expecting you to come here today. I've also been expecting you to bring the cavalry, which Demming told me you planned to do. Did you think I would, in light of those facts, stand here with Demming, one gun between the two of us, and simply wait for your arrival? Perhaps you thought I would serve tea and cakes when you got here?"

Lancaster suddenly gave a shrill whistle.

Just as suddenly, eleven of his men appeared. Some stepped out from behind trees. Some rose from behind boulders where they had been crouching. All were armed either with rifles or revolvers. All their guns were aimed at either Ki or Jessie.

"I'm so sorry you didn't see fit to accept my business proposition, Miss Starbuck," Lancaster said as he began to raise his left hand.

He's going to signal his men to begin shooting, Jessie thought. She glanced at Ki.

Understanding passed between them although no words had been spoken.

Jessie fired a round that had been deliberately aimed to go over Lancaster's head. It caused him to drop his arm and go for his gun. As his gun cleared leather, Jessie shot it out of his hand.

During the few seconds that had elapsed between her first and second shot, Ki had seized Demming from behind and was holding him in a chokehold with his forearm braced across the man's throat. Before the sound of Jessie's second shot had faded, he kicked out, his foot catching Lancaster in the buttocks and sending him tumbling down to the ground.

Jessie bent and scooped up the gun Lancaster had dropped as he fell while Ki maintained his grip on Demming who was desperately struggling to free himself.

"You try shooting at us," Ki yelled to Lancaster's men who were still training their weapons on him and on Jessie, "and this man dies." To Jessie, he muttered, "Move to the southeast. There are no gunmen stationed there. If we go that way, there's little or no chance of either of us getting shot in the back."

Jessie did as Ki had told her to do.

He backed up, Demming kicking and clawing at him but still his prisoner. "When we get to those rocks behind us, take cover," he told Jessie. "Meanwhile, stay close behind me so you don't make a target for these jaspers to practice on."

"Take them!" Lancaster roared.

172

"We can't, boss," one of his men yelled back. "We'll drill Demming if we try to."

"I don't give a tinker's damn about Demming!" Lancaster roared even more loudly.

"No!" a horrified Demming screamed.

A shot sounded. Then another.

"Run for it!" Jessie shouted to Ki as both rounds buried themselves in Demming's body, causing it to jerk spasmodically and causing a scream to rip from the man's lips before it was cut off in mid-voice by death.

Ki let go of Demming. The man fell to the ground. Ki went running after Jessie who was heading for the rocks in the distance, turning and firing as he ran. Both of them pursued a zigzag course designed to keep them out of the paths of the many rounds Lancaster's men were firing at them.

The sound of gunfire filled the area. The smell of gunsmoke tainted the air.

Ki's foot caught in a root that ran along the surface of the ground for a few inches. He lost his balance and fell.

"Ki!" Jessie cried in alarm. She turned and started back toward him.

The din increased as Jessie reached Ki and helped him to his feet. Neither of them, as they began to run again for the shelter of the rocks realized at first what had caused the sudden increase in the noise level.

But then, "Look!" an excited Jessie shouted.

Ki looked to his left and saw eight troopers led by Lieutenant Stowe come galloping into the camp.

Several of Lancaster's men began firing at the soldiers who promptly dismounted, turned their horses over to two of their number, and returned the fire.

"Jessie!" Stowe shouted. "This way!"

She beckoned to Ki and ran toward where Stowe remained aboard his mount in the midst of the melee. When she reached him, she leaped up behind him, and he spurred his horse and went galloping toward the rocks. Once there, Jessie got down from his horse and took cover. A moment later, after securing his horse in the rear, so did Stowe.

"I'm sorry," he told Jessie, trying to catch his breath.

"Sorry for what?" she asked, bracing her gunhand on the large boulder in front of her and taking aim at one of Lancaster's gunmen.

"For being too personal."

"I don't know what you're talking about." Jessie squeezed off a shot that caught her target in the left shoulder and caused him to let out a loud yell and duck back behind a tree.

"I should have called you Miss Starbuck, not Jessie," Stowe explained sheepishly.

Jessie couldn't help it. She burst into laughter. "Forget about it. Right now we have more important things to worry about. Like that slick so-and-so over there who's trying to sneak up on us."

Stowe fired at the man who was slowly creeping toward their position. He scored a direct hit. The man dropped like a stone and moved no more.

"What are you doing here?" Jessie asked Stowe. "I thought Major Lane was dead set against giving me any help in this matter we're faced with here."

"He was and is. I told him I heard rumors that there were some Dog Soldiers about to break camp on the reservation and head back north to their home ground. I told him I thought I ought to look into the matter. He agreed. So I got my men together and sent eight of them to the coulee you told me about and brought the rest here to see if you needed any help. It appears that you did—and do."

"That, Lieutenant, is the understatement of the decade." Jessie gave the man by her side a smile and then, turning away from him and scanning the area, asked, "Where's Ki?"

"I don't know. He was running beside my horse when

you and I headed for these rocks, but it seems he never did get here with us."

Fear chilled Jessie. Not for herself but for Ki. She scanned the cow camp but saw no sign of him anywhere. Had he taken cover somewhere? Had he been hit and fallen during the gun battle in a spot where she could not see him?

Around her, troopers had taken cover wherever they could. Two crouched some distance away behind a rotting deadfall. Another soldier had taken up a position in a clump of birches from which he was firing steadily. The other troopers had deployed themselves farther away. Jessie could not see them, only the occasional burst of flame from their gun barrels.

"Lancaster and his men have us outnumbered," a dour Lieutenant Stowe commented. "It will be getting dark soon. Once it does, we can attempt a retreat."

"You can retreat. I'm not retreating. Not without Ki."

"Even with that one man I shot out of action for good, Lancaster still has the superior force. Before arriving here, as I told you earlier, I sent eight of my troopers to the coulee where you found the stolen stock. When it gets dark, I'll send one of my men to get them. Once they arrive here, we can rendezvous with them in the rear. Then we can mount a truly formidable attack on Lancaster's forces with far greater chance of success than we have now."

"You don't think Lancaster will just sit still in the meantime while we're camped out somewhere waiting for your other eight men to join us, do you?"

"That's not the point—"

"It is the point. For me, it is. I'm not letting him get away from me. And I'm not leaving here until I know what has happened to Ki."

"Miss Starbuck, you are without a doubt a most exasperating woman."

"Then take your troopers and go and do what you think you have to do so you won't be bothered by me."

Stowe hesitated a moment. Then, "I am bothered by you, Miss . . . Jessie."

She looked at him, saw the light in his eager eyes, saw him nod wordlessly in affirmation of what he had just said. "I shall take that as a compliment, Lieutenant."

"David."

"David."

"It was meant as one but expressed rather crudely, I fear."

Jessie smiled faintly and then ducked as a round whined over her head.

Stowe eased down beside her and put his arm around her. Then he kissed her.

She responded by putting down her gun and wrapping her arms around the man to whom she had been attracted since the moment of their first meeting.

As their kiss continued, Jessie's lips parted to admit Stowe's probing tongue, which slid between her teeth and began to explore. As she sucked on it, it probed more deeply. Desire flooded her. She held Stowe tightly against her yearning body as his hands began to explore her.

Around them, guns still fired, and gunsmoke still blurred the air. But where they were, lost in their own private world, there was only bliss.

That other world, the ugly one encircling them, was momentarily forgotten as they fumbled with their clothes and then with each other's hot bodies. It seemed to Jessie that Stowe took an eternity to penetrate her but penetrate her he did only minutes later. She received him with a welcoming joy and pressed herself against him, her wet lips exploring his neck, his throat, his face.

They lay hidden in the brush behind the boulder both from their attackers and from Stowe's troopers. The Lieutenant pounded down upon Jessie, and she thrust eagerly upward to meet him, rhythmically matching his passionate onslaught with one of her own.

They climaxed simultaneously, their moans of pleasure blending as ecstasy caught them in its erotic web.

Afterward, they lay side by side, both of them gradually returning to earth from the heights of the sensuous heaven they had just scaled together. Gradually, they became aware of the occasional gunshot that broke the relative stillness that had settled on the camp during their encounter.

"I've wanted you since I first saw you," Stowe murmured, kissing Jessie's closed eyelids before beginning to dress.

She sat up and also began to dress. "It was good."

"The best."

Jessie's next words were lost in the loud noise made by the pounding hooves of many horses.

She hurriedly finished dressing as Stowe resumed his former position at the boulder that served as a barricade.

"What is it?" she asked him.

"Damned if I know what it is!" a puzzled Stowe answered.

"It's Brave Buffalo!" Jessie cried. "Those men riding with him must be the Dog Soldiers!"

"Why are they attacking us?"

"They're not. Don't you see?"

"See what?"

"They are attacking Lancaster and his men, not us. They've come to help us!"

A baffled Stowe could only stare with disbelieving eyes at the Cheyenne who were rampaging through the camp, firing their guns at Lancaster's cowhands as they overran and successfully routed them.

Two of Lancaster's men went down and died as they tried frantically to flee from the Indians, one from a bullet in the brain, the other from a Cheyenne lance that impaled him against the trunk of a blackjack oak.

At the moment that Brave Buffalo and the Cheyenne who were riding with him invaded the cow camp, Ki was in the process of silently stalking his prey—Lancaster.

Earlier, as Jessie and Stowe made their ride for cover, he had chosen to put into action a plan that had been forming in his mind almost since the battle had begun. The confusion generated by the arrival of Stowe and his troopers, not to mention the wild orgy of shooting, gave him an opportunity to execute his plan.

He had raced away from Jessie and Stowe and taken cover behind the four horses in the care of one of the lieutenant's troopers. Then, his eyes roving over the scene unfolding around him, he spotted Lancaster in the distance. The man had somebody else's gun in his hand now, having lost his own earlier. He was firing with wild enthusiasm but without much effect.

One of his men must have given him that gun, Ki speculated as he judged the distance to his prey and noted the positions Lancaster's men had taken relative to their leader. Well, I'm the one to take that gun away from him, Ki thought grimly.

He remained concealed behind the horses for another minute, ignoring the startled look the horse-holder was giving him. Once he was sure of his plan and had calculated all the potential impediments to it, he darted out from behind the horses and sprinted, not toward Lancaster but away from him.

When he reached an outcropping of rock, he circled around it and continued running until he was at the other end of the rocky formation, approximately fifty yards, he judged, to the rear of Lancaster and the two men nearest him.

One of those men was several yards behind and to the

right of his employer. The other man was on his left and about even with him.

Gathering and concentrating all the energy in both his mind and body, Ki relaxed. Then, amid the shouting and the smoke and the sounds of snorting horses, which were the audible emblems of the pitched battle being waged in the camp involving cowhands, Indians, and soldiers, he began to move stealthily forward, his *ninja* warrior's heart hungry for the fray.

He was halfway to Lancaster when the man on Lancaster's right turned and began to thumb cartridges out of his gunbelt and place them in the empty chambers of his revolver.

Ki froze.

But the man had spotted him. He raised the barrel of his newly loaded gun, gripping it in both hands.

Ki swiftly removed one of the *shuriken* from the pocket of his vest. He threw the five-bladed metal star just as the cowhand facing him thumbed back the hammer of his gun.

The *shuriken* spun through the air on its deadly mission. It neatly split the man's left eyeball from top to bottom as it cut through bone on its way to his brain.

As the man slumped forward and fell lifeless in a heap on the ground, Ki moved swiftly forward. But, before he could reach Lancaster, the cattleman jumped to his feet, shouted to the man on his left to run for it, and began to do just that himself.

Ki changed course and went after Lancaster.

"Boss, look out!" the man with Lancaster yelled as he spotted Ki.

Lancaster glanced over his shoulder, saw Ki, and got off a snap shot. The round keened harmlessly past Ki's left ear as he ran on.

The man with Lancaster also fired at Ki and missed. Ki swiftly dispatched another *shuriken*, and the man who had just tried to kill him went down and didn't get back up. He couldn't get back up because life had left him.

"Stop! Lancaster!" Ki shouted above the continuing din. "If you don't, you're a dead man!" Another *shuriken* appeared in his hand.

Lancaster came to an abrupt halt and turned to face Ki.

"Drop your gun!" Ki ordered.

Fear flooded Lancaster's face as he saw the *shuriken* in Ki's right hand and the other one in the body of his dead cowhand. He dropped his gun. He raised his hands. His voice cracked as he asked, "Are you going to kill me?"

Before Ki could answer him, Jessie ran up and asked, "Are you all right?"

"I'm fine."

"I was so worried about you. Where did you go?"

"I went after Lancaster. Got him too."

Jessie gave Lancaster a stony stare. "I heard what you just asked Ki. I think he should kill you. But he won't. You'll hang for what you've done, Lancaster, and I only wish I could be the one to spring the trapdoor and send you on your way to hell."

Brave Buffalo rode up to them. "I take this one. Put him with other bad men."

"Before you do," Ki said, "I want to ask him a question." Turning to Lancaster, Ki said, "You knew that Jim Hanson was stealing Indian horses, didn't you?"

Lancaster hesitated a moment. Then, with a somewhat shaky show of his former bravado, he answered in the affirmative. "It was another way to make some money. Hanson split the money he got for the horses he stole and sold in Dodge with me. Fifty-fifty. It was a business matter, and I am, after all, a businessman."

"You *were* a businessman," Jessie pointed out.

Lancaster's face fell. His show of bravado collapsed as Brave Buffalo marched him over to where the would-be cattle baron's men, those who had survived the battle, were being carefully guarded by Lieutenant Stowe's troopers.

"It's remarkable, isn't it?" a thoughtful Ki commented.

"What is?"

"The way the Cheyenne and the cavalry cleaned up this operation. With a little help from us, of course."

"It just goes to show what can occur if people work together instead of fight each other."

"There's one thing about all this that I don't understand, Jessie. Why did Brave Buffalo and his riders jump right into the middle of this fracas? What brought them here in the first place?"

"I asked Brave Buffalo about that once the shooting had stopped. He told me he had seen us passing the Darlington Agency after leaving Fort Reno. He said he wondered at the time why we had no soldiers with us. He guessed, correctly, that the army had refused to assist us. So he rode back to his camp, rounded up his Dog Soldiers, and then trailed us here. He said he thought we might need some help in handling Lancaster and his gunhawks. He was only too glad to give it to us."

"I want to go thank him for that," Ki said. "I also want to thank Lieutenant Stowe for his help."

"I'll go with you. I want to thank them both too."

When Jessie and Ki, together with Brave Buffalo, arrived at the Darlington Agency the following afternoon, they found Agent Amos Butler engaged in conversation with Lieutenant Stowe.

"Excuse me," Jessie said, "I didn't mean to interrupt."

"Come in, come in, Miss Starbuck," Butler exclaimed, rising and rounding his desk to shake hands with Jessie, then with Ki, and finally with Brave Buffalo. "Lieutenant Stowe has just been telling me what heroism you all displayed yesterday during the apprehension and detention of Mr. Lancaster and his cohorts. He told me he retrieved and returned your herd to you, Miss Starbuck, and that he has sent Lancaster and his men to Kansas under military guard to stand trial there for the terrible evil they have done. I congratulated him, and I now take the opportunity also to congratulate the three of you as well on an important job very well done. Won't you be seated? Lieutenant Stowe and I had just begun to discuss how much beef would be needed by the agency for the next distribution to the Indians."

"That's one of the reasons I came here today," Jessie said as she took a seat. Ki and Brave Buffalo seated themselves on either side of her.

"What is on your mind, Miss Starbuck?" Butler asked as he returned to the chair behind his desk and sat down.

"I've discussed the matter of the army requisitioning beef with other cattle owners, and we have an alternative proposal to make, Mr. Butler. It is this. Suppose we agree to supply you, on a pro-rata and monthly basis, with all the beef you need."

"Why, that would be nothing less than wonderful," Butler enthused. "It would eliminate our need to enlist the aid of the army in our efforts to acquire the beef we need. I'm sure such an arrangement would make everyone very happy."

"It would most certainly make me happy," Stowe declared. "I've not relished my recent rancorous confrontations with cattle owners."

"What price would you charge us, Miss Starbuck, you and the other owners?" Butler inquired.

"We would sell you our stock at the same price the government is offering to pay at the time of sale."

"You would save much money," Brave Buffalo told Butler. "Beef contractors cheat you."

"Surely that is not so," Butler objected. "The beef contractors we have done business with on occasion recently have charged us ten cents per pound less than what the government was paying cattle owners such as Miss Starbuck."

"But contractors' beef cost you more because they keep cattle from water until time to sell them to you," Brave Buffalo stated.

"I don't understand."

The Cheyenne said, "Beef contractors bring cattle to Canadian River. Let them drink much water there. Then they bring them across river and you weigh them. They much fat cattle then. So you pay high price mostly for water in cattle's bellies."

Ki burst out laughing and then, noticing Butler's embarrassed expression, apologized for his outburst.

"That's quite all right, Ki," a chastened Butler said. "I deserve to be the laughing stock I obviously am for not having better managed the affairs of this agency."

"I have something to say on that point," Jessie said. "You know, don't you, Mr. Butler, that your assistant, Mark Demming, was killed yesterday in the gun battle at Lancaster's cow camp?"

"Lieutenant Stowe has so informed me. Evil as that man was, I would have wished him a kinder fate."

"You're now in need of an assistant to replace Demming, is that not so?"

Butler nodded. "Yes, I am obviously in dire need of an able man to keep me from making more of a fool of myself than I already have in this office."

"I have just the man for you."

"You have? And who might that be?"

Jessie reached out and placed a hand on Brave Buffalo's shoulder. "This man would make a competent assistant administrator of the agency, with your help and guidance."

"My word!" Butler exclaimed, leaping up from behind his desk and coming around it to pump Brave Buffalo's hand. "What a wonderful, what a truly worthy suggestion! It shall be done! Brave Buffalo, from this time forth, you shall be the assistant agent of the Darlington Agency." Butler paused in his enthusiastic shaking of the Cheyenne's hand. "You will accept the position, won't you?"

"I will," Brave Buffalo said without hesitation.

"Now it's my turn to make a suggestion, Mr. Butler, if I may," Stowe said. When Butler turned expectantly to face him, he continued, "Why not employ Brave Buffalo's Dog Soldiers as a contingent of Indian police, such as those found at other agencies? They can serve this agency under his leadership."

"Capital idea! We do sorely need such a force. With it, we will have far less reason to trouble your Major Lane for help in keeping the peace here, Lieutenant. Is such an arrangement acceptable to you, Brave Buffalo?"

"It is."

"Then you've got yourself a fine army now," Stowe told Butler.

"There's not a man among them," Ki said, "that I wouldn't want siding me in time of trouble, Brave Buffalo very much included."

"I second that sentiment," Stowe said sincerely.

"So do I," Jessie said just as sincerely.

Butler glanced at the banjo clock on the wall and exclaimed, "My goodness, it's supper time already. If you will all join me, I'm sure this is one supper that will be a most festive occasion."

They did and it was.

Watch for

LONE STAR AND THE MOUNTAIN OF GOLD

eighty-fourth novel in the exciting
LONE STAR
series from Jove

coming in August!

From the Creators of Longarm!

Featuring the beautiful Jessica Starbuck and her loyal half-American half-Japanese martial arts sidekick Ki.